MW00817883

# Reyes's Raina

## Heroes for Hire, Book 17

## Dale Mayer

## Books in This Series:

REYES'S RAINA: HEROES FOR HIRE, BOOK 17
Dale Mayer
Valley Publishing Ltd.

Copyright © 2019

All rights reserved. Except for use in any review, the reproduction or utilization of this work in whole or in part by any electronic, mechanical or other means, now known or hereafter invented, including xerography, photocopying and recording, or in any information storage or retrieval system, is forbidden without the written permission of the publisher.

This is a work of fiction. Names, characters, places, brands, media, and incidents are either the product of the author's imagination or are used fictitiously. Any resemblance to actual events, locales, or persons, living or dead, is entirely coincidental.

ISBN-13: 978-1-773361-22-2
Print Edition

## About This Book

**He once picked the wrong woman... he won't make that mistake again.**

Reyes Drere came from a long line of gardeners. He'd known since he was little which way his life was going to go and it had nothing to do with planting seasons. When he joined Legendary Securities after eight years as a Navy SEAL he'd been avoiding going home and joining the family business.

The family business included an ex-fiancé he had no wish to see again. Her sister was a good friend but there was nothing more dead than a dead love – unless it was a dead ex-fiancé...

Raina is reeling from the shock of seeing the only man she's ever loved showing up at work one day, his new boss in tow. Ice is all about plants on a grand scale, whereas Reyes appears to be all about denial.

Only the shocks continue as her twin and Reyes ex-fiancé show up dead... and he's the one with a motive...

**Sign up to be notified of all Dale's releases here!**

http://dalemayer.com/category/blog/

# Your Free Book Awaits!

## *KILL OR BE KILLED*

Part of an elite SEAL team, Mason takes on the dangerous jobs no one else wants to do – or can do. When he's on a mission, he's focused and dedicated. When he's not, he plays as hard as he fights.

Until he meets a woman he can't have but can't forget. Software developer, Tesla lost her brother in combat and has no intention of getting close to someone else in the military. Determined to save other US soldiers from a similar fate, she's created a program that could save lives. But other countries know about the program, and they won't stop until they get it – and get her.

*Time is running out … For her … For him … For them …*

**DOWNLOAD** a *complimentary* copy of MASON? Just tell me where to send it!

http://dalemayer.com/sealsmason/

# Prologue

REYES DRERE STRETCHED out his legs in his assigned seat.

"So, who's next?" Dezi asked Reyes.

They sat beside each other in the commercial airplane. Harrison was two rows up, working on his laptop, and Anders had stayed behind in London for a few more days with Angelica.

Reyes shrugged, "No clue, but I doubt it'll be me."

"Yeah? Why's that?" Dezi asked.

"Not interested. I don't think it's fair to go off and leave somebody worrying if I'm ever coming home again."

"But we're in a different life now," Dezi said. "I might have agreed with you before, but we're not in the same dangerous line of work."

"Yeah? Look at the last job. Bullets and accidents were all over the place."

"Sure," Dezi agreed. "But that doesn't mean it'll continue. A lot of the jobs Levi's company handles haven't been dangerous at all. So, yes, on this London job, there were a couple accidents, a couple bullet wounds, but nothing terribly serious."

Reyes chuckled. "You realize, if anybody else heard us, they couldn't possibly understand."

"I know, right? It's a whole different world now."

"Besides, nobody's in my life. Although I'm doing a lot of jobs for Levi these days, I can't say I've met anybody in particular who appeals."

"That's the weird thing about this," Dezi said. "It's almost like you go on a job, and it's got your name written all over it."

"I'm traveling with Ice next week. She wants to get some special tropical plants for around the pool area at the compound."

"With the Texas heat, they'll probably thrive." He looked at Reyes. "Why you?" Dezi sat up straight in his seat at that thought. "Interesting."

"What's interesting about it?"

"That she asked for you. It's not like we're any different. I don't know why the boss lady wants you to go with her," Dezi said.

"Don't get your nose out of joint. It's probably because of my family's background."

"What background is that?"

"Gardeners," Reyes said succinctly. "We've got a large business, growing and importing plants for gardening stores."

"So your family grows the annuals shipped to those gardening places in time for spring and summer planting?"

Reyes nodded.

"Wow. Never occurred to me somebody would do that by hand."

"It's hardly manual work anymore," Reyes said. "My family's business is pretty big. A lot of it is automated now."

"So Ice thinks you might know which ones to pick?"

Reyes shrugged. He didn't know how much to tell Dezi. Then he figured the truth was best. "It's more a case of she asked about my family's business, so I told her some things. Then I talked to my family, and now I'm taking her there. She'll meet them. We'll talk about what will work, what won't work and will arrange for transport of whatever she buys."

"Okay, that's a different story." Dezi relaxed in his chair. "*Transport*? Are you guys flying or driving?"

"We'll probably both fly there together," Reyes said. "She'll fly back alone because I'm returning with the truckful of plants."

"That's a lot of traveling."

"Sure, but we'll keep them environmentally stable enough."

"Is she really buying a truckload?"

Reyes looked at his buddy sideways and then chuckled. "I think she's planning on bringing back a *huge* truckload."

"Like a three-ton truck?"

"Like an eighteen-wheeler," he said, laughing. "But I don't know. We'll see when we get there."

"Okay. So, considering you're going home, and obviously that job has your name written all over it, have you got an ex-girlfriend back there who you're planning on seeing, maybe falling in love with?"

"Nope," Reyes said. "My ex and I broke up a couple years ago." He had said that in a light tone, but it didn't stop the pain on the inside. It had been a long time, but still that betrayal ate at him. His family kept him up to date on her health and welfare mostly because he had never told them the truth.

"What's the former girlfriend's name from back home?"

Reyes looked at Dezi in surprise. "Why?"

Dezi just shrugged with a grin. "Curious. So give.

What's her name?"

"Her name is Reana. She has a twin sister, Raina." He twisted in his seat on the plane, so he could look at Dezi, seeing the big grin on his friend's face. Reyes growled. "What's so funny?"

"I'm just thinking about the way a lot of the names of the couples have worked out, as everyone paired up. Look at North and Nikki, Anders and Angelica." Dezi settled into his seat. "Just saying, looks like you're next."

Reyes shifted away and ignored his friend. Dezi didn't know the truth. Reyes had no intention of ever getting back together with someone who had betrayed him. What was that saying? *Fool me once, shame on you; fool me twice, shame on me.* And that was how Reyes felt about *that* relationship. It was over. It was dusted. It was done.

Now the twin sister though …

No, that was just asking for more trouble.

# Chapter 1

R EYES GOT OFF the flight, walking at Ice's side, heading to where their ride awaited them outside the San Diego International Airport. It would be a strange trip, coming back home.

"Are you sure you're up for this?" Ice murmured at his side.

"Absolutely." He gave her a bright smile. "At some point you have to face your past, whether you like it or not."

She nodded and said, "If I'd realized that your ex-fiancée was involved in the family business, I wouldn't have asked."

"So it's a good thing you didn't know," he said cheerfully. "She's moved on. I've moved on. That's life. Besides, she's an accountant, and the gardening center is just one of her many clients."

"I had no clue your family was majorly in the greenhouse business."

"It's been the family business for a long time," he said. "I was always one of those kids getting my hands dirty in the gardens. My grandfather is just like me. We have tropicals we import from seedlings, but they're really not profitable in the long run. A bunch of them we bring in just because they're fun, just because they're part of what makes up this gardening passion, something we want to keep doing. If you follow your passion into a big business, it's important to keep feeding that part of you that started the whole thing."

"I totally agree," Ice said. "It's why Levi and I do what we do."

Reyes's lips twitched. "I'm not trying to save the world. I was just happy to save one plant at a time."

Her laughter pealed out across the airport crowd. People turned to look. She was a stunning figure. With her long blond hair and that confident stride, she strode forward, like a Viking Valkyrie. Reyes never admired another woman quite as much. He loved her goal-oriented *I can handle anything* attitude.

Outside the airport, he stopped and took a deep breath. Beside him, Ice murmured, "Far cry from Texas, isn't it?"

He nodded. "I suppose it has its own charm. I've been away from San Diego for just long enough now that the noise, the traffic, the pollution, the people ..."

She chuckled. "It's one of the reasons why Texas was a good fit for us. We needed the space. The space and the privacy from the world at large. The land around us provided a bit of a buffer, a bit of a balance between what we do and where we live."

Reyes nodded. "That makes perfect sense to me. All the years in the military, ... you see so much. Your life is ordered from one direction to another, from one moment to the next. When I started working for you, it was like being free again. Coming back here now, this almost feels like a jail cell."

"That's just because it's different, because you're not used to it anymore," Ice said. "Give it time. You'll adjust."

He smiled. "Would you ever move back here? I know your father lives here."

"I come back and forth to visit him. But, with all the

traveling I do, I'm happy to stay in Texas."

"What about your dad? Don't you miss him?"

"Of course I do," she said with a bright smile. "But, if there was ever a man who was as busy as I am, it's him. We're both cut from the same cloth. The two of us have our passions, and we put 100 percent into them."

Reyes nodded. "I'd like to meet him," he announced.

"You will later tonight," she said. "We're staying with him."

He glanced her way. "I thought I was supposed to find my own accommodations."

She turned to him in surprise. "As far as you're concerned, this is a job. All expenses are on us."

He frowned.

She stopped and looked at him in understanding. "Unless you have friends you want to visit?"

He shook his head. "Not yet. Maybe in a day or two but, right now, no. I don't know what kind of reception I'll get."

"From your mom? Surely she'll be incredibly delighted to see you."

"True," Reyes said. "So will my father. I always got along well with him. It's just a little awkward."

"This is the first time you've been back since the breakup?"

He nodded. "Yeah, it is. So, awkward times ahead."

She linked her arm through his. "Nonsense. It will be fine," she said, looking at her watch. "Once our driver arrives, we'll be at the garden center for about four hours this afternoon. Then my dad will pick us up, and we'll have dinner with him. Is that okay with you?"

He smiled. "Absolutely."

Together they meandered through the crowds, looking for the vehicle that would pick them up. Behind him, Reyes heard a voice call out his name. He turned to search in that direction and saw his brother. Immediately his arm shot up in greeting. He and Ice made their way toward him.

As soon as Reyes was face-to-face with his brother, all his fears and worries fell away. Their arms opened, and the two hugged each other with the same warmth they'd always had.

Then his brother stepped back and gave him a clap on the shoulder. "Damn, it's good to see you."

Reyes nodded. "Right back at you." He studied his brother, the older brother who he'd spent so much of his time chasing, trying to be just like him. "You don't look like you've aged a day."

"Oh, I've aged a lot of days," Ron said. He turned to look at Ice, and his eyes opened in appreciation. Immediately he had her hand in his. "I'm Ron Drere, Reyes's older brother."

Ice shook his hand. "I'm Ice. Nice to meet you."

Ron chuckled. "My mom's talked about nothing else since she heard you were coming. We're supposed to be very nice to you because you're Reyes's new boss."

Reyes rolled his eyes. "You don't *have* to be very nice to her. She's a sweetheart, so you'll be nice just because she is a person you *want* to be nice to," he said gently.

Ron laughed, peals of joy ringing out over the crowds. "Come on. Let's get out of here. The traffic at this airport seems to get worse every year."

"I'm surprised you're the one who came to pick us up. No employees free to come?"

"Hey! I volunteered for the job," Ron said. "If you were still living at home and took off for a week or two, maybe not, but I haven't seen you in two years. So I wanted to see you again. Besides, it's time."

Reyes had to agree. It was time. He slapped his brother on the back. "You're right. It is."

They ambled toward the closest parking area and, sure enough, found one of the pickups that belonged to the center. "I see we don't get any fancy treatment while we're here," he said with a chuckle.

"Wanted to make you feel at home," Ron said. "No point in beating around the bush. We are who we are." With Ice sitting between them on the bench seat, he pulled out of the airport and onto the highway headed toward the family's gardening center.

Reyes stared out at the traffic and shook his head. "I'd forgotten," he said.

"How could you? It hasn't been that long."

"But the last year plus," Ice said, "you've been traveling for us. And, when you returned, it was to the wide open spaces to help you rest and recuperate."

At her wording, Ron turned to look at her. Reyes understood his brother really didn't know what kind of work he'd always done, the stress on the body and the mind from seeing so much devastation. "True enough," he said to Ice. "And I think that part has been one of the biggest benefits."

"Not to mention the rest of it," she said with a big smirk.

He chuckled, thinking about the food, the friends, ... the family. "Isn't that the truth?"

Ron picked up the conversation, asking Ice, "So, you're part of Legendary Security?"

"Levi and I started the company," Ice said comfortably, then added thoughtfully, "along with two of our best friends,

Rhodes and Merk. They've been with us since the beginning."

"And Stone?" Reyes asked. "Wasn't Stone there in the beginning?"

She laughed out loud. "Well, he was, and he wasn't. Stone is missing a leg," she said by way of explanation for Ron. "He was a bit of a bugger for not listening to us about getting off his leg, so he was assigned to office duty more often than not as a punishment when he overdid things. But, yeah, he's been at the core since the beginning. Now we're like eighteen strong, maybe even twenty."

"And that's just the men," Reyes said, smiling. "I highly doubt any of the women would consider they weren't part of it. They don't all work for the company, but, with all the apartments and the families, it certainly feels like they are part of it."

"Not too many of you aren't paired up now," Ice added thoughtfully. "You and Dezi are it, now that Anders and North both bit the dust ..."

Ron looked over at Reyes. "Really? You don't have a girlfriend?"

There was silence in the truck for a long moment, then Reyes said smoothly, "No, no one full-time."

Ron didn't say anything to that, which was a good thing. Reyes didn't want to get into a discussion as to whether he was still pining for his ex-fiancée. The answer to that was a flat-out no. He wasn't. But she was a very close friend of the family, and he didn't want to get in the middle of the old arguments again. It had been one of the hardest things when they'd split. How did you explain to everyone why you split when they all loved her, when nobody could see anything wrong? And, even if some had seen the cracks, they didn't say anything to him about it. Of course what was wrong within a relationship wasn't always obvious from the outside. He'd found it easy to just walk away and to leave her to give whatever explanations she wanted.

Ron then said something that made Reyes wonder exactly what Reana had said. "She said she didn't think you'd still be carrying on with the same girlfriend."

Ice turned to look at him.

He looked down at her and gave a short shake of his head. Then he turned to stare out the window. But he couldn't let it go. "Not sure what *same one* you're talking about. The only woman in my life back then was my fiancée."

Again an uncomfortable silence filled the cab.

Ron, his tone disbelieving, asked, "Seriously?"

Reyes gave a heavy sigh, leaned forward and looked at him. "I don't know what she told you, but I certainly wasn't having an affair. There was not another woman in my life."

Ron caught up to the heavier traffic and gave him a hard, fast look. "That's exactly what she said, that she caught you in bed with another woman and broke it off."

Reyes snorted. "Really?"

Ice leaned over and gently patted his knee. He wasn't sure if it was encouragement or just being supportive. Then he realized he didn't give a damn who wanted the truth after all this time. He was tired of lying.

"Somebody was caught in bed with another woman," he said quietly, "but it wasn't me."

A strangled sound came from his brother's throat. He understood instantly. Ron looked over at him. "Are you saying Reana was in bed with another woman?"

"Yes. And I didn't recognize the woman. There was no

mistaking what they were up to." He sank back in the seat and stared out the window.

Under his breath, his brother muttered, "Jesus."

"Exactly," Reyes said. "Somehow I figured nobody would know *that* part."

Ice chuckled. "Everybody says what they need to for self-preservation. Don't blame her for trying to save her own skin at an uncomfortable moment. Blame her for how she let everybody else think about you in the ensuing years, yes. But, at that moment, it was just about survival."

Reyes had to think about that for a moment. Then he realized how true it was. He couldn't blame Reana for what blurted out of her mouth when she was caught in that situation. But he sure as hell could blame her for what came afterward—or failed to be cleared up later. Some things were just inexcusable.

RAINA WOODCROFT WALKED through the greenhouse. A brand-new shipment of pansies had come in, and they'd wilted. She kept the temperature a little on the cooler side to help them recover and watered them with a gentle rain wand. She wanted water tables for them, but they hadn't gotten set up in this area.

As soon as the pansies recovered, they'd be moved to the general sales area. This area was more of a rest-and-recuperate section of the greenhouse. She had the ability to open windows at the top to let out the heated air to regulate the temperature. She kept a close eye on the plants that were under a lot of heat stress.

She worked away, humming gently to herself. Of all the things she enjoyed, being around the greenery was at the top of her list. These plants meant something to her. Every one mattered. Then again, to her, all of Mother Nature mattered. She wasn't so big on the men she knew, but the plants, the animals, the birdlife, she was totally okay with those. Including reptiles and insects.

She was probably the only one in the place who wouldn't immediately kill a spider. Some of the spiders did great work, and she went to extreme lengths to save them when she could. She usually got called whenever an infestation was found somewhere, so she could move them out. And she did so with joy. Even though they were the least loved of Mother Nature's critters, they were still worthy of saving, as far as she was concerned. She knew not everybody agreed, but apparently she was an oddity.

It was partly caused by growing up with a twin—a twin who was a lot more exuberant, a lot more in-your-face, a lot more driven to get what she wanted. They'd been really close when younger, but mostly because Raina had never really fought her sister's dominant role. Raina suspected that, in every case, one twin was more dominant than the other. In her case, she was the less dominant one. She was much more laid-back about everything; her sister was more aggressive, always needing to be right. She had a lot of really good qualities, but she treated people more as disposable commodities.

When Raina had heard Reyes would arrive here today, it had brought back a flood of memories.

It still hurt to realize her sister and Reyes had had the opportunity of a lifetime, and Reana had blown it. Raina didn't understand what had gone wrong. She'd heard her sister's version, but it was hard for her to believe that Reyes would have treated Reana like that.

Raina wanted to believe her sister. But sometimes she was a liar when it suited her. Raina remembered when they were both in the same history class. She had been blamed for something her sister had done, and her sister let her take the blame, even though Raina had protested profusely. The teacher and her sister had gone against her. Raina hadn't failed the course, but she'd had to redo a major project just so she could pass, and she never did get the appropriate marks for it. Her sister thought it was funny as hell. After that Raina made sure she was never in the same class as her sister.

The counselor had struggled with that because the school offered a limited number of courses. So Raina had gone an entirely different way than her sister. Her sister was all about making sure she was somebody, whereas Raina was all about making sure she was her own person. It was okay to be quiet. It was okay to be one of the less exuberant personalities. But she wanted to be authentic—whoever she was to be. Her sister had said she was foolish, that authenticity was for the birds.

The problem was, Raina had been half in love with Reyes herself. But, of course, her sister—the brighter light of the two of them—had been the one who had attracted his attention, with Raina always in the background. But she'd refused to let that hold her down. She'd found her own friends, her own relationships, and she'd turned her back on both of them. She'd been happy for them as long as they were happy.

But they were a combustible couple. They fought a lot—and made up noisily—so the whole world would know. Her sister was incredibly demonstrative and loved public displays of affection. She was also a huge drama queen.

Reyes didn't appear to be as comfortable with any of that but was happy to go along with what Reana wanted.

Raina, on the other hand, was quiet. She would hold hands in public and maybe give a hug, but she wasn't into passionate displays of kissing or fondling, which her sister was all about. It was more for show, at least Raina thought so, than anything else, but that was being mean to her sister.

She stopped, turned to look around the greenhouse where she worked and, with quiet satisfaction, saw that the plants were recuperating. This was where Raina belonged, dealing with plants that needed her, dealing with animals that needed her. When younger, she'd wanted to be a vet but had given up that dream when her grades hadn't been quite good enough. Maybe if she had tried harder. But she'd seen kids with that natural intelligence which she didn't seem to have.

She'd been really sad about it for a long time. She'd tried her damnedest and still couldn't seem to get the marks. She was a solid B student. Getting an A was always an overjoyed moment. Reana, on the other hand, seemed to be an A student. Somehow she got the looks, the brains, and the personality.

Only after working with plants did Raina realize her true love was nature and that she had a special affinity with plants in particular.

Raina gently stroked the soft petals of an African violet. The fuzzy tops always intrigued her. Kind of like her and her sister's relationship. There was that outside view of most people—when you rubbed up against them, you were pretty sure you knew exactly who they were. But, on the inside, they were very different people. While Raina and Reana looked the same physically, Reana went to great pains to act differently than her quiet sister. Raina herself rarely did anything to distinguish herself from her sister, knowing her sister would do it first. Raina was just happy to get up in the morning, run a brush through her hair. She would braid it or put it in a high ponytail. She rarely wore makeup and never gave a damn about looking her best. Why? Anybody who mattered would see her for who she was.

At least that was what she hoped.

It hadn't worked out that way with Reyes. But now she was too entrenched in the idea of being herself, not dressing up or presenting herself to be anything other than who she really was. Maybe if she had an office job or worked in sales or in any media-related position, she would have taken more care with her appearance. But the truth was, she was wrist deep in dirt half the time, bending over plants, digging and transplanting them on a regular basis. Nobody gave a damn whether she had on mascara and lipstick or not.

Her sister used to laugh at her and tell her that she was just a garden grub. And maybe that was the truth, but Raina was happy with her lot in life. She and her boyfriend had broken up a few months ago, and that was okay too. Maybe it was sad, but what had been sadder was the relationship itself. They'd just been chugging along, as if waiting for somebody more exciting to come into their lives. It had hardly been gemstones and roses, and definitely passion was not there. After one of those *Hey, where are we going with this?* conversations, they had broken up.

"Raina?"

She turned to see Annemarie—her boss and Reyes's mother—standing in the doorway, a phone in her hand. "What's up?"

"Reyes is about ten minutes away," she said, her words

causing a big smile to break out on her face. "Are you okay to handle the front desk, so I can spend some time with him?"

# Chapter 2

"**O**F COURSE I am," Raina said calmly. Inside her heart leaped. It wasn't an emotion she would let everyone know about.

Annemarie had been delighted when Reana and Reyes had gotten engaged. Thinking it was a perfect pairing. Raina never understood. She herself had been worried but figured that ultimately they would handle their problems. Unfortunately they had.

Raina walked into the store and realized that everybody must be away on lunch break because normally at least half a dozen people could be seen working. She glanced at Annemarie. "Where is everyone?"

Annemarie raised both hands and shook her head. "A birthday party or something. A bunch of the employees wanted to lunch together. I said yes because, at the time, it was dead in here. But now look at it."

Raina surveyed the chaotic line and stepped up to one of the registers to ring customers through. She didn't care what she did when she was at work. Whether it was handling customers or dealing with plants, she was willing to do whatever was needed. Her preference was to stay in the background, but the business had grown exponentially in the last few years, and it was hard to keep full-time staff.

She lost herself in the heavy traffic of the noon rush.

When no more customers were in front of her, she finally took a break and stepped back with a big sigh of relief.

"What are you doing working the register?"

The male voice was one she readily recognized. She lifted her gaze to Reyes. A grin slid out. "Wow. You finally came back to the slumlands, did you?"

Reyes's lips quirked, and that endearing smile he had peeked out. It used to make her heart ache. "It's all good. I'm back with my boss to pick up a very hefty order of plants for Texas."

"Surely there are plants closer than this," she said.

He shrugged. "Possibly. But she's pretty interested in getting some of the plants here and trying to get them to grow there."

"Still, would be easier to get them closer to home," Raina warned. "You know how hard it'll be to transplant some of them." One of the most stunning women she'd ever seen stepped up beside Reyes. She was tall and slim, with an almost foreign air to her. She looked to be such a capable can-do woman that it was hard not to admire her right from the get-go. Raina realized this had to be Reyes's boss.

She reached out a hand. "Hi, I'm Raina, an old friend of the family."

The woman smiled and shook her hand in a firm grip. "I'm Ice. Reyes's boss."

Raina chuckled. "Good for him. I always enjoy seeing guys like him under a woman." She said it in such a teasing voice that no one would take her words seriously.

Ice's grin was infectious, and her laugh was charming. "That's all right. He fits in with all the rest of the guys and women back home. Back to the plants. Do you really think I'll have that much trouble transplanting some of these?" she asked as she crossed her arms and stared out the window at the many greenhouses. "We were planning on taking a truckful back. Of course we do have a lot of heat in Texas, so I was thinking our weather would be similar to California weather. Although Texas is drier."

"There'll be a lot of similarities," Raina said, "but you'll have to watch the humidity and moisture. It is a long trip. Did you consider that?"

"That's why we have a reefer truck standing by. Still, I'm torn between flying home or riding back with Reyes in the refrigerated transport," she said.

Raina tilted her head at that. "If you can keep the temperature cool enough without chilling the plants, they'd probably be okay." She tapped her chin as she thought about it. "It's an interesting conundrum. All plants will have a certain amount of stress with the move. You're completely changing their climate, and some of these are tropical. But then, as you know, Texas has a lot of heat. I've never really worked in that climate before, so I don't know the full ins and outs of it."

Reyes looked at her. "How have you been, Raina?"

She shrugged, mustering up a bright smile. "I'm doing good. Still working here."

"Good. This is where you belong," he said firmly. "More than anybody else I know of, this is your type of environment."

She shrugged again and chuckled. "I do prefer plants over people." She glanced at Ice to see the older woman studying her intently. She smiled. "Are you keeping Reyes in line?"

Ice gave a definitive nod. "Hard not to in my world. We all follow orders, whether we like them or not. It's what keeps us safe."

Raina thought that was an odd statement, but then she didn't know much about what Reyes was doing now. If it was as dangerous as what he used to do, then she understood.

Just then a commotion was heard at the front door. She turned, and her heart sank. "Damn," she whispered under her breath. She looked up, caught Ice's narrowed gaze, gave a half-ashamed smile and whispered, "Sorry."

Reyes reached out, his hand coming down on her shoulder. "Things haven't improved?"

"Nope," Raina said brightly as she watched her sister storm toward her. "And not likely to either."

And suddenly her larger-than-life, burning-hotter-than-a-flame sister was here. Reana pulled her arm back to get a full swing at Reyes's face. When her hand connected with his cheek, the sound of the *crack* could be heard across the room. Then there was silence.

IF HE'D SEEN her hand coming, he might have stopped her. As it was, it had come out of the blue. He'd forgotten just how volatile Reana was. He placed his palm to his cheek, feeling the burn from her blow. Grimly he glared at her. "I see you're just as nasty as you always were."

His ex-fiancée gasped as her back straightened. "What the hell are you doing here?"

"That's enough out of you," Annemarie said from behind them. "That is my son. This is my place of business. He is always welcome here. You, if you don't know how to behave yourself, are not."

Raina almost smiled at that. Annemarie was many

things, but she was no pushover.

Suddenly she was there between her son and Reana.

Reana lifted her chin, her nose in the air, and glared at Annemarie.

But Annemarie was not daunted. She glared right back. "I suggest you go outside and cool off. When you know how to behave again, you may step back into this store. In the meantime, keep your melodramatic actions to yourself." When Reana still didn't move, Annemarie lifted her arm, pointed at the front door and, in a hard voice, said, "Go."

With a huff and a swing of her long hair, Reana stormed out the front door.

Instantly the air calmed. Annemarie turned to look at Raina.

Raina shrugged and said, "Sorry."

Annemarie sighed. "I keep telling you how you *must* stop apologizing for your sister. She is who she is, and you are who you are. You are not responsible for her actions."

"I know you keep telling me that," Raina said, "but some things are just instinctive."

Annemarie turned to look up at Ice and then at Reyes. When she saw her son's cheek, she winced.

Reyes looked at her and smiled. "It's not the first time she's hit me, you know."

Annemarie nodded slowly. "At first I thought you two would be great together but did worry she'd be too volatile for you. The fact that you picked a woman who would beat the crap out of you, and you would take it, always worried me," she muttered.

"I remember you pushing us together," Reyes said in surprise. "Not that you were worried about us. You were certainly angry when we broke up." He shrugged. "Besides, she was always volatile. Ever since she was little."

"Yes, but you're the only one who let her hit you," his mother said in exasperation. "What the hell is wrong with you that you would do that?"

Reyes felt the old anger spark through him. How dare she question that when his father had been taking his mother's shit all their marriage. "What would you like me to do?" he asked coolly. "Hit her back?"

His mother fisted her hands on her hips and glared at him.

He sighed and said, "This is why I don't come home. Within five minutes of being here, you're telling me off." He motioned at Ice. "Let's finish our business and go home. At least there I feel welcome." He turned and walked out.

Outside he stopped and took several deep breaths. Since his ex-fiancée had gone out the front door, he'd gone out the back. Some things just never changed. His mother was forever criticizing him, telling him how he should be more of a man, and yet, it wasn't in him to fight back with somebody as difficult as Reana. The problem was, Reana was like his mother. He'd seen her hit his father more than a time or two. The fact that his father hadn't hit her back was good, but he was surprised his mother had no respect for either of them. For a long time Reana had held Reyes's heart in her hands, and she'd squeezed every drop out of it. When he'd found her in bed with another woman, the relief had been overwhelming. He'd had a solid reason for walking away. And he'd taken it.

He hadn't explained to anybody what had happened. But to think that was how his mother still saw him was really irritating. He stared out at the greenery with the sunshine beating down, taking several deep, long, slow breaths. When a male voice washed over him, he sighed and turned to face his father.

His father studied Reyes's face for a long moment. "So, your ex-fiancée or your mother?"

A grin slipped out. "Both?"

His dad smiled. "Unfortunately there's an awful lot of similarity between the two of them. The thing is, volatile, high-spirited, passionate women don't understand men who are calmer, quiet, and not full of drama. It took me a long time to figure out how to handle your mother. I don't think you had enough time with Reana to figure it out."

"No, I didn't," Reyes said. "Thank God."

His father laughed. "Good point. We worried about you when you were engaged. She's many things, but she's not easy."

"Considering that relationship is over and done with, why don't we find something more pleasant to talk about?" He motioned at all the greenhouses lining the sides of the property and the acreage that stretched out in front of him. "I can't believe you're still growing this business."

"I can't believe it still needs to grow," his father said. "Our bottom line has doubled in the last three years alone. The supply is incredible, and we're having trouble keeping up with the demand."

The two men walked down the aisle, comfortably switching their discussion to business, away from the unpleasant topic of women. They'd never been much for father-and-son talks. Reyes had been the youngest, a little bit less sure of himself, following his big brother around, who always seemed to know everything and exactly what he wanted to do. Finding his own way had been a little harder for Reyes. It was one of the reasons he'd joined the navy.

He'd become his own man while he was in the service.

Maybe there he'd gained enough confidence to make him feel like he could handle Reana, and that was one of the biggest mistakes of his life. "Why does Raina still work here?"

"Why not?" his father asked. "We'd be lost without her. She's the best damn worker we've got, and she's the only one who understands plants the way she does. She's better with them than both your mother and I am." His father looked at him. "Why the hell couldn't you have picked her over her sister?"

"I might have," Reyes said, "if she had ever showed me any interest. She was my first choice, but she ignored me. Her sister seemed to think I was something worth going after. When she did, I fell into her grasp. Feels very much like a butterfly into a spiderweb now, though."

His father laughed out loud. He punched his son gently on the shoulder. "At least you've grown up and freed yourself from that mess."

"I have indeed." He looked around, then turned toward his dad. "What about Raina? Is she married? I didn't see a ring."

His father looked at him for a long moment, then shook his head. "Interesting that you even looked."

Self-consciously, he shrugged. "Hey, it's been a couple years since I was here. Of course I looked."

"Well, no one is in her life now. She's not showing any interest in settling down."

"Is my ex?" Reyes asked in a dry tone. "She just belted the hell outta my face back there." He reached up to touch his cheek.

His father's gaze narrowed. "Again?"

"Yeah. Again. I didn't even see it coming this time," he said. "Two years later and my reflexes apparently have slowed when it comes to registering her attacks."

"That girl needs to watch herself," his father warned. "If she hit me, I'd be really hard-pressed not to hit her back."

"Really? You've never hit Mom back." He laughed when his father rolled his eyes; then the laughter died.

"And yet, your mother is still judging me for it." His words held deep regrets.

Reyes realized his mother was who she was, but it was still frustrating.

His father nodded. "Yeah, she's not gotten any easier either. Although Annemarie and Reana are usually best of friends, they've had a few arguments. Once Reana raised her hand to hit your mother. Your mother threatened her with a lawsuit, and Reana seemed to step back. I think both your mother and Reana are probably frustrated that you won't find a way to stop both of them yourself."

"And maybe I should," Reyes said. "But honestly I can't be bothered. I'm only here for a couple days. I had hoped to make it a fun, peaceful two days, to see everybody before I head home again."

His father shoved his hands in his pockets and rocked on his heels. "I'll be sad to see you go. It's kind of nice to have you around."

"Yeah, but, as you can tell, I don't belong here," Reyes said, something settling deep inside him. "You know what? I wasn't sure about being in Texas, but, now that I'm back here, if nothing else, it's made me realize San Diego isn't home. I'm more than happy to leave again."

"Don't hold it against your mother, son."

Something unsettling was in his father's tone. Reyes

turned to look at him. "No, I won't. She is who she is, and, as long as the two of you are happy together, then I guess that's what I can hope for. But she's just as abusive in her own way as Reana is." He walked off with a shake of his head. When he reached the far end of the greenhouse, he turned to see his mother standing beside his father, a shocked look on her face.

He shrugged and walked on. Maybe it was time for the truth to be told. He didn't know. Everybody in the family thought Reyes had the perfect relationship with both his parents. But Reyes was more like his father, and sometimes he only saw his father as a long-suffering husband. Reyes thought a lot of love must be there for his father to stay through all the abuse. But, as Reyes saw Reana again, he was just damn happy his life had gone in a different direction. He wanted peace in his world. Passion too. But he didn't want all the pain that went with living with certain people.

# Chapter 3

RAINA TRIED TO keep herself busy. She'd heard way too much of the family dynamics—both hers and his. But then she wasn't new to any of it. She'd often wondered how Reyes had stayed at home as long as he had. But then she'd often wondered how Harold had stayed married to Annemarie too.

Annemarie had mellowed with time. Raising two sons had probably been better than raising daughters. Reyes's older brother, Ron, had had enough temper to fight back. But Reyes was like his father, a gentle giant.

Raina wondered how Reyes had fared in the military, if the bullying had been bad there too. She'd often wondered if he would grow up to be a man with a backbone because, as a kid, he'd taken the brunt of Annemarie's temper. But Raina was proud to see he stood tall and firm today.

Even when her sister had belted the hell out of his face, there hadn't been that instinctive flash to strike back.

He'd taken it and just looked at her with cold disdain. True, his mother had stepped forward and had snapped at her sister this time, but then that was the way it had always been. The years in the navy had been good for him. And obviously Ice held a lot of respect and admiration for him. For that Raina was glad. Growing up in the Drere household had been hard on Reyes. Everybody thought that, since the family business had been a success, then the family was also a success. But she often thought Reyes got the raw deal. Harold and Harold's father, old Ben, who was still around and still putted up and down the property, were very much like Reyes. They survived by being quiet and forceful in their own way—but never aggressive.

Then again she understood. The Drere family situation was very similar to the living conditions with the Woodcroft sisters. It had been exhausting. Raina had chosen to go the quiet route, to find peace in her own world, in her own time, in her own way. But it hadn't been easy, and it hadn't been fast. It was funny because she'd always assumed she and Reyes would be better friends than her sister and Reyes were—had hoped for more, in fact—but that almost deadly attraction between Reyes and her sister had made it even harder to watch.

It seemed that the minute her sister had understood Raina's interest, Reana had been all over taking Reyes away from Raina. At the time Raina figured it was her own fault because she hadn't fought for him but quickly realized he hadn't even seen her anyway, like the two of them were together in a darkened room. When her sister had stepped into the relationship, it was like all the lights had turned on for him.

Raina had to admit to a little quiet satisfaction when it all fell apart, but she'd gone her own way and hoped they'd both healed and moved on. She still loved her sister.

That didn't mean she liked her very much.

But nothing Raina could say would make her sister change.

The end of the day was finally drawing to a close. She closed out the registers and locked the front door and headed into the back room to check on her plants. She set the temperature on the thermostats and closed the overhead greenhouse vents, gave them one extra mist, then walked out toward her vehicle.

As she approached, she watched a limousine pull up. Ice and Reyes were waiting for it. A man got out of the back and hugged Ice.

The two men shook hands. Trying not to watch, and finding it hard not to, Raina smiled as they all got into the back seat. It seemed Reyes had finally landed on his feet. First the navy and now with Ice's company. Raina was happy for him. It also reminded her of how far she hadn't come.

She'd worked for the Drere company since she was a teenager. She'd been more like a puppy following behind Ron and Reyes growing up. Her presence had almost been taken for granted, like part of the furniture. She hated to even think of it that way, but it was hard not to. Now she had her own arborist license, worked as a private contractor and consultant for a couple big tree-pruning-and-cutting companies in town, and yet, she worked here at the garden center still.

She was a little lost, figuring out where she wanted to go and what she wanted to do. All she knew was that she needed to keep working with plants. That was where she found her peace. That was where her soul smiled. Something about seeing Reyes again, how he had finally settled into something for himself, made her realize she needed something better for her own future too.

As she got into her car, her sister ripped through the parking lot again. Reana still handled the company's accounting. She'd started years ago, when she was a student in bookkeeping; then she'd gone on to get her CPA.

Raina hated bookkeeping; she preferred to sit among the trees in the back property for her breaks and have nothing to do with people. Harold and Ben used to join her, bringing out cups of tea, sitting down, discussing the latest black currants or the new hollyhocks that were coming.

Years ago Reyes had joined them—whereas Ron and Annemarie would be in the front, dealing with customers, talking, laughing, and joking loud and proud.

But then that was what the world was all about. It took many kinds.

Sighing heavily, she got into her vehicle and drove home. She lived in a small apartment a half mile away. Often she walked to work. Reana had a big brownstone of her own, but then she made a lot more money than Raina did. Money was important to Reana, much less so to Raina.

When she got inside, her mother was already calling on the phone. She did it every day to make sure her daughters got home. "I'm home, Mom," she answered. "Everything's fine."

"Is it though?" her mother asked worriedly. "Your sister called. She's horribly upset. She said seeing Reyes was terrible."

"I don't know how it could have been," Raina said quietly, hating how her sister had to blow everything out of proportion. "She didn't even give him a chance to say a word, and she smacked him hard across the face. Then she and Annemarie got into yet another spat, and Annemarie ordered Reana off the property."

Her mother gasped. "I don't think that's quite true. She said she argued with Reyes outside first."

Raina pinched the bridge of her nose. "I don't think so, Mom." The trouble was, she really didn't know herself because one of the gifts that Reana had was confusing the issue with half lies and small truths. "She just walked in the front door, took one look at him and hit him. I was standing right there, Mom."

"Well, we can't be thinking that of your sister now, can we?" her mother said in a soothing voice. "You know how upset she can get."

"I do," Raina said. "But I'm really tired, Mom. If you don't mind, I'm going to make myself some dinner."

She hung up before her mother had a chance to argue. Raina did not want to go over the day's events. It seemed like she'd spent her life dealing with Reana's issues. Her mother used to call Raina all the time to discuss all the terrible things in her sister's life, asking why wasn't Raina doing more to help her sister.

The trouble was, Reana had caused all this, and it wasn't Raina's job to fix it. But it had taken her a long time to figure that out. And, now at twenty-seven, she figured it was well past time for her sister to handle her own crap.

REYES SHOULDN'T HAVE been surprised at the appearance of the limousine. He knew Ice's father was a doctor with his own private clinic. The introductions had been easy and quiet. He really liked Ice's father. The man was knowledgeable, capable, and obviously adored his daughter. The two of them had very similar features, but Ice was a more feminine version, and her father was steely gray-haired now versus Ice's Viking blond looks.

Dinner was a royal affair at his home, with a manservant and a house that rivaled any movie star's. "Your place is truly beautiful," Reyes said sincerely. He picked up his glass of wine. "Thank you so much for letting me stay here."

Ice's father laughed. "Nice to be appreciated but you're more than welcome. Most of the Legendary Security team has stayed here at one time or another. Anytime cases in California arise, I always open my doors. At least that way I get to see my daughter sometimes." He sent a knowing look in Ice's direction.

Apparently she wouldn't be swayed. She grinned at him. "We talk on the telephone all the time," she said. "Besides, if I'm supposed to come here more often, then you have to come my way more often too."

He rolled his eyes. "Now if only I could get away from the business."

"Exactly," she said gently. She held up her glass of wine. "To making the most of these moments."

They all gently clinked their glasses together.

"Do I understand that you're here just for plants this time?" her father asked in amazement.

Reyes chuckled.

"Yes. I'm fixing up the big outdoor pool area," she said, "and I wanted to do it right."

"Are you sure it wasn't an excuse to return to California?" her father teased. "You know what? If you want, you can take the plane back, and we can fly the plants home."

She stared at him in surprise. "What plane? Do you have a plane now?"

He shrugged self-consciously. "Well, it's not really mine but …" He let his voice trail off.

She glanced at Reyes. "It'd be easier on the plants, wouldn't it?"

He nodded slowly. He didn't live in a world where people had their own planes, particularly one big enough for a huge order of plants. He faced Ice's father. "Sir, what size is the plane? I think Ice is hoping for some rather large plants."

He raised an eyebrow at his daughter. "Are you going higher than ten feet?"

Ice pursed her mouth, turned to Reyes. "Are we?"

Reyes shook his head. "They'd be too hard to transplant. As it is, we'll need Bobcats for some of them."

She thrummed her fingers on the table. "Let me think about it. A flight would be a lot faster, and I wouldn't have to worry about the health of the plants so much."

"But you said you were supposed to take the reefer back for somebody?"

She waved a hand in the air. "I've got lots of guys who could drive it back. It would save us a long trip and be better overall for the plants. Let me take a look, Dad. What size plane and how much cargo space is there?"

He laughed. "There's lots. I highly doubt you'd come even close to filling that space."

She gave him a look of satisfaction. "Great. In fact, perfect," she said. "So that's probably a yes."

He smiled. "I'll tell the pilot he can plan a trip to Texas in the near future."

She glanced over at him. "You might as well come back with us. You can spend the night, see the place, and you can fly home the next day … or two."

He looked at her in surprise, lifted an eyebrow and said, "You know something? I think that's a hell of a good idea."

Reyes smiled. It would be fun to see these two together at the compound. After his day, Reyes would be more than happy to get back home to Texas and to forget about this visit—forever.

# Chapter 4

RAINA SETTLED INTO her couch, her feet up on her coffee table, her laptop open on her legs and the TV on. It seemed like she needed multiple distractions tonight, and still nothing worked. Her mind kept returning to the look on Reyes's face when her sister had slapped him. There was anger, a cold disdain, but, more than that, there was almost a world weariness.

Reana was many things, and *temperamental* was just the start.

Raina had known that, once Reana decided to go after Reyes, there wasn't a hope in hell of him looking at Raina. And she'd been right. It was so typical of every male on the planet. Reana's stunningly incredible figure and her vibrant personality with passion oozing from her made her come alive like no one else.

Raina had heard of other people having passionate and enticing mouths, huge expressive eyes, facial features that twisted and turned with every movement. And she imagined that some potentially Italian- or Mediterranean-born women had those same mannerisms. But Raina hadn't seen anyone similar to her sister.

It was exhausting to live with her. At least for Raina. Their mother seemed to flourish in that environment, even though she was more like Raina than her outgoing twin. And

Raina again wondered how Reyes had handled that. All the men since Reyes had moved on seemed to be completely blindsided and stood with goofy smiles on their faces whenever Reana had walked past them. And that had been Reyes's reaction initially too. But that goofiness hadn't lasted long. He'd settled in with a long-suffering look on his face after a while. Raina had wondered about that. How did one walk away and still retain who you were? Because staying in that abusive relationship and retaining who you were wasn't an option.

The phone rang again. She stared down at her mother's number and groaned. This was the second call tonight.

But her training—a lifetime of being at her mother's beck and call—had her reaching for the phone and hitting Talk. "Mom? What's the matter?"

"Have you heard from your sister?" Worry was evident in her tone.

Also a different note of *something* made Raina sit up and take notice. "No, I haven't, but then why would I?" she asked. "We rarely talk. You know that."

"She's not answering her cell phone," her mother said. "You know she lives on that thing."

"She might have turned it off," Raina said. "She might have left it at home. She might have had a fight and left it in a restaurant." Raina smiled at that. "She's done that a couple times. Remember?"

"I know. But nobody is answering. In both those instances somebody at the restaurant answered for her."

"True, but you can't expect other people to do that every time. In this case, it's possible somebody stole the phone. I don't know. But I doubt anything is wrong."

"You don't know that," her mother said, almost with a

note of desperation. "Something's wrong. I can feel it."

Raina pinched the bridge of her nose. She closed the lid on her laptop and turned down the volume on the TV. At least this way she could hear her mother better. "Why? What's telling you something is wrong?"

"She was really distraught earlier," her mother said. "You know that's not like her."

It was all Raina could do to hold back a snort. Her sister was *always* like that. "Did she tell you why she was upset?"

"She kept saying, *He's back. He's back.* And how bad that would be for her."

Raina's stomach sank. "Who was she talking about?" Inside she knew though. It had to be Reyes. He was the only person she knew who was suddenly back. Although both sisters had known he was coming. For Raina it had been a good thing, but obviously for her sister it wasn't. "I presume she meant Reyes, but why should she care?"

"I asked her that too," her mother said. "And she just kept saying that I didn't understand. How I didn't understand."

"Didn't understand what?"

Raina hated to think something really dark was between her sister and Reyes. Raina had always really liked him. As much as she had trouble with her sister, Reana was essentially a good person. *Mostly.* So it didn't make sense that something was wrong in that corner. But, at the same time, if her sister was truly distraught, then something was going on somewhere.

"I know. I know," her mother said. "But she just kept repeating it over and over again."

"Any idea why she would be upset that Reyes is back?"

"Well, they were engaged to be married," her mother

said in exasperation. "Isn't that enough?"

"No, it's not," Raina said, trying hard not to get upset. She was more than fed up with all this drama. "Even if they were engaged, it's been two years. You know Reana has had multiple boyfriends since then."

"She never got over him, you know?" her mother said quietly. "She told me that. Everybody else was just a substitute. I still don't like it. I'll hang up and try her again."

Her mother ended the call, leaving Raina sitting here with her phone in her hand. She frowned at it, wondering what was going on now. It was possible her sister had gotten herself into a spot of trouble. It wasn't that she lived dangerously, but she had made enemies.

As Raina sat here, she brought up a word document on her laptop and wrote down all the men and the problems in Reana's life. It was a fairly long list of boyfriends she'd dumped. Some were completely devastated, and some had begged her to take them back. Others had been angry. A couple had even posted pretty nasty things about her on Facebook. But none of them were recent events. So Raina didn't know what the hell her sister was up to now.

Instinctively she picked up the phone and dialed her sister's number. It went to voicemail. Raina left a message. "Hey, it's me. Mom's having a fit, thinking you're in trouble. Do you want to get back to us please?" She hung up.

When the phone rang ten or fifteen minutes later, she was surprised to see her sister's phone number on the screen. "Reana?"

"Yes," her sister said in a hard voice. "Get Mom off my back, will you? I'm in trouble, and I don't want to drag her down with me." And just like that she hung up.

Raina called her back and again got voicemail. "What

kind of trouble? Can I help?"

This time her sister didn't return her call. Raina phoned their mom and gave her a sweetened version of the message from her sister, saying, "Look. She answered my voicemail. She's alive. I don't know what's going on. She said she's in some trouble, but honestly I don't know that we can do anything to help."

"But you heard her voice?" her mother asked in relief. "So she is okay?"

Raina hemmed and hawed over the term *okay* because who knew if her sister was okay or not. Her words had been disturbing. Had she meant them that way? She didn't know how else to be but dramatic.

"I can only assume that. She didn't ask for any help, and I did call her back and leave her a message, asking if I could do anything," Raina said. "Let's give her a chance to solve whatever is going on. Then we'll take it from there."

"Okay. Good," her mother cried out in relief. "At least you heard from her."

The trouble was, Raina heard from her sister again and again that night. But each time she'd answered the phone, the connection would die, or Reana would hang up. Unnerved, Raina didn't know what to do. She also didn't know who to call. Definitely not her mother.

Either somebody had Reana's phone and was playing with it, or she was in trouble and whatever call for help she was trying to get out wasn't working. Finally Raina ended up phoning another old friend.

When Vince answered, she said, "Hey. I know this is a voice from the past, but I guess I'm looking for advice."

Vince chuckled. "You're lucky you caught me. I just came back from a trip to Thailand."

She smiled. "Lucky you," she said enviously. "And, hey, did you know Reyes is in town?"

"Holy shit! Is he?" Vince asked in surprise. "Damn. I'll have to see if I can meet up with him for breakfast or something."

"That would be good. He's not planning on staying long."

"He told me how he was working in Texas now, so I'm surprised he is here in California."

"His boss is redoing a massive pool, outdoor solarium area, and they came looking for plants."

At that, he chuckled. "Trust Reyes. Even though he doesn't work for the family company anymore, he is still plugging the business."

"Yeah. Anyway," she said quietly, "I'm calling about my sister."

"Yeah? What's that bitch up to?" he asked in a friendly voice.

She grinned. "You haven't changed, have you?"

"Has she?"

At that, Raina winced. "No, she hasn't. The trouble is, she's being a little difficult right now. I'm not sure if she's in any serious trouble." She quickly relayed the series of events that happened tonight.

"And how many times has she called when you got no voice at the other end?"

"Three," she said, "and I have to admit that I'm pretty unnerved by the whole thing."

"With good reason," Vince said. "What's her number?"

She gave it to him.

"Look. I'm not sure what's going on, and there's not a whole lot I can do, but let me make some calls."

"Will do," she said. "And thanks, Vince."

"Don't worry about it," he said. "We go way back. And, damn, it'd be good to see Reyes again. How about breakfast, the three of us?"

She hesitated and then shrugged. "If he's up for it, I am."

"Have you seen him?"

"Yeah, he came into the store today."

"Good," Vince said. "I'll give him a shout and set up breakfast. I'll get back to you."

"Sounds good." And she hung up.

Now all she had to do was wait. And hope her sister didn't make any more strange phone calls. And that Vince could get somebody to look into it. But she knew that, from a police perspective, there wasn't anything to look into. At least not yet.

REYES SAT IN the living room, enjoying a glass of whiskey with Ice and her father. It had been a great evening. Reyes had learned a lot about Ice and her family. It was another plus, working for Levi and Ice. Reyes really did feel like he belonged there.

When his phone rang, he pulled it out and murmured, "Sorry." He stood and took a few steps away, realizing it was Vince. "Hey! Where are you?"

"I'm in San Diego," Vince said with a chuckle. "I just spoke to Raina. She says you're in town."

"I am. You've been doing so much traveling, I wasn't sure that you'd be here at the same time I was."

"It's not like you gave me any dates to work with."

Reyes chuckled. "Since when did dates ever matter to

you? You come and go at will."

"Well, not any longer," he said. "Things didn't work out this last trip, so I'll be looking for another job again."

Reyes winced. "I'm sorry about that."

"Since I left the navy, it's been a lot more difficult to make a living than I expected. I keep thinking people will be out there who I'm willing to work for, but it turns out they end up sucking as humans."

Reyes understood. He'd been another of those who preferred to work with honest and trustworthy people. When it came to many big corporations, too often the bosses were the actual corrupt ones and took their team down a path they did not want to go down.

"How about we meet for breakfast? I'd really like to see you."

"I can do breakfast," Reyes said. "I don't have any wheels right now though."

"I'll pick you up," Vince said. "Give me an address."

He gave the address to Ice's father's house.

"Wow. Living high on the hog, aren't you?" Vince asked.

"Not really. I'm here with Ice. She's one of the bosses at Legendary Security, and we're staying with her father."

"Nice. How about seven o'clock tomorrow morning?"

"That works."

Vince hesitated. "Hey, I half invited Raina. Do you have a problem if she joins us?"

"I'm totally okay if she joins us," Reyes said in surprise. "Is something going on between the two of you?"

At that, Vince's laughter pealed out through the phone. "Nope. Not my type. She's always been a kid sister to me. And her sister is sheer poison. As you found out. That's why

Raina contacted me tonight." He launched into an explanation of what was going on with Reana.

Reyes listened to Vince's monologue for a long moment. "Are we thinking something is seriously wrong?" he asked curiously. "I don't know who she is anymore, but that doesn't sound like her."

"Raina seems to be worried, and I know their mother is. The trouble is, there's not a whole lot we can do."

"We can triangulate where her cell phone is coming from, and, if she happens to be at home, it's easy enough to take a quick drive-by to make sure she's okay."

"Good point," Vince said.

Reyes turned to look around. His laptop was somewhere nearby. He spotted it and said, "Give me her phone number, will ya?"

Vince recited it and then waited.

Reyes typed in the number and then worked on triangulating where the calls had come from. He'd learned a lot of tricks in the military, but working for Legendary had increased his skills and kept him updated in the technology arena.

He realized he'd caught the attention of Ice and her father.

Ice stepped toward him, a frown on her face. "Something wrong?" she whispered.

He looked up with a grimace. "Maybe. Reana ..." he said. "She could be in trouble."

Ice sat down in the chair beside him and watched as he worked on the laptop.

"Vince, her phone is on and says she's at home."

"What do you want to bet it's just her being her old self? What's her address?"

Reyes gave him the address per the map. "She's still in the brownstone condo, I believe."

"That's only a couple blocks from me. Do you want me to run by and make sure she's okay?"

"If you wouldn't mind, that would be good. If I go, and nothing is wrong, it'll just start World War III," Reyes said with humor. "But, if you go, it won't upset her."

"Well, stand by. I'm only ten minutes from giving you a callback." He hung up.

Reyes slumped in his chair, studying the flashing dot on his laptop.

"Is that where she lives?" Ice snagged the laptop from him, magnified it larger so she could take a look at how far away the address was from their location. "What exactly is going on?"

Reyes filled her in. "As difficult as Reana can be, this isn't normal behavior for her."

Ice snorted. "With any woman, it's hard to understand what their cry for help is all about. You know that her slapping you today was another cry for help. She's a very unhappy woman."

Reyes stared at his boss in surprise. "Reana has always been on top of the world. She would be very angry if you were to tell her that she's unhappy."

Ice shot him a hard look. "I understand women. I understand men too. But I really understand women. And your Reana is a very unhappy woman. And, if something ugly is going on, this could be a cry for help."

# Chapter 5

S HE COULDN'T SETTLE. Raina got up, sat down, got up, walked around, sat down again and finally picked up the phone to call her sister once more. This time no answer was followed by no voicemail. Which usually meant the message box was full. Raina walked over to the small Juliet balcony outside her living room and stared in the direction of her sister's home. "Should I walk over there and make sure you're okay?"

She hated to. Her sister would be absolutely furious for Raina's intrusion if nothing was wrong. For all Raina knew, Reana had a brand-new boyfriend and was playing some weird game. Her sister was into games, in bed and out. She used to laugh at Raina for being a *vanilla* sexual partner, according to her terminology.

"You don't know what you're missing," Reana had said with a chuckle. "But maybe, when you get out of your frozen skin, you'll find out there's so much more to life."

Raina hadn't risen to the bait. Usually when her sister said stuff like that, she was pushing to get a reaction. But, if this was another game, it was a desperate one. And it was upsetting a lot of people.

She phoned Vince back. "Sorry. I couldn't wait."

"I'm approaching her house," Vince said. "I talked to Reyes. He pinged her phone, and it showed it was still at her townhome."

"Oh, good," Raina said. "I hate to think she might be playing games, but ..."

"I'll call you back when I get there." He hung up.

She knew she should have waited. It was her sister after all. She sat back down and waited. And waited. But there was nothing. No call from Vince; no call from Reana. Raina thought about what Vince had said about Reyes and worried.

And then suddenly Reyes called. "Vince has gone into Reana's townhome. There was no answer at the door. He picked the lock and went through the whole house, inside and out, but there's no sign of her. Her phone was sitting on the kitchen counter, but her purse is missing and so are her keys."

Raina sagged on the couch, running her fingers through her hair. "Sorry. I should have thought about her leaving the phone behind." She groaned. "I'm just edgy right now," she said. "I don't understand what's happening."

"None of us do," he said quietly. "And that's why Vince went in. He shouldn't have because it was locked. But ..."

"I would have let myself in too," she said quietly. "Thank you for checking."

"He also said how we were set to go for breakfast in the morning. Are you okay with that?"

"I am if you are." Her tone was a little divided. "It's kind of hard to see you again."

"It was hard coming back," Reyes said. "It's not been easy."

"I'm sorry about my sister. That was very uncalled for."

He laughed. "Sure, but, if she doesn't cause a scene, it's not her, is it?"

He said it in such a smooth, natural tone that she realized he wasn't angry anymore. She smiled. "Hey, I'm glad you're not upset at her for it."

"There's no point now. I took a lot of shit from your sister a long time ago. There's a reason I walked. She hasn't changed her opinion of me since then either."

"Good," she said. "In that case, breakfast would be nice."

"Vince is picking me up a little before seven. Did he mention a place?"

"No," she said. "I'll send him a text and ask where to meet you guys."

"See you in the morning then." Reyes hung up.

She wondered at her instinctive sense of loss. It was one thing if it had been so many years ago when she still held a torch for him. But she'd gotten over that once he'd been engaged to her sister. Raina had worked long and hard, just to get her emotions in control and to break off from Reyes, so his upcoming nuptials to her sister wouldn't hold Raina back. She'd been surprised, almost horrified, when they had announced their news, but Raina had dealt with it.

Now that he was back and single, she wasn't going down that trail again. Something about knowing he'd been with her sister made Raina want to avoid him completely. But she and Reyes had been friends since they were kids. Good friends for a long time. And she didn't want to lose that. And, if she were honest, that spark remained inside her when she spoke or saw Reyes. But to go down that path and to lose him again wasn't a pain she was willing to bear a second time.

Like he'd said, it was hard to come back and to pick up the pieces, hard to find that natural rhythm in a friendship again. And, if he was trying, well, she had to do her best to try too. He was a good man.

She put away her phone and prepped for bed. Her last thoughts as she curled up with her head on the pillow were about her sister. Why would Reana have left her phone behind? And, if she had, who the hell had made all those strange calls? If Reana had made them, why wouldn't she have taken her phone with her?

With nothing making sense, Raina pushed it all away. Not much about her sister's life made sense.

Raina slept, but she slept rough. She kept surfacing, checking her phone to see if her sister had contacted her, then fell back under again. Her dreams were filled with tormenting laughter from the many years living with her beautiful yet sometimes obnoxious sister, mixed with some memories of her sister's boyfriends who Raina had met over the years. Some had cried on Raina's shoulder, hoping maybe she could somehow repair the damage done to their relationship with her sister. As if hoping Raina would go to bat for the men and that her sister would forgive them for whatever imagined transgressions they might have made. But her sister went through men like she went through clothes. They were fun and fashionable for a little while, and then she dropped them and moved on. She was a fashionista in a way most women never got a chance to try.

Raina had watched so many men fall at her sister's feet, only to end up in puddles of devastation. That had been very difficult. But something about her sister's relationship with Reyes had made her sister angrier, as if she couldn't force him to do her will. And he'd been stalwart, never defending himself but never giving her the rise she wanted. One particular dinner, where everybody had been gathered for a barbecue, her sister had been at her finest, flirting with everybody, then daring Reyes to tell her off. He just raised an eyebrow and said that, if she chose to not be with him, then that was fine; he'd move on too.

He hadn't said it in a way that would publicly humiliate her or him, but he'd said it quietly when she'd come back to him yet again with a taunting smile on her face, asking if he cared.

Raina just happened to be behind him at the time. She thought his response had been odd. But maybe not—considering how absolutely difficult her sister had been. Raina had tried to tell Reana that she was embarrassing her fiancé. Her sister had smirked and said, "When we pick a fight, my dear, the making up is that much better." She'd patted Raina on the cheek and wandered off, tossing back, "When you grow up, you'll understand."

It had horrified Raina. And then made her wonder if that was really what this was all about—sex games.

When she finally awoke the next morning, it was already six-twenty. Her eyes burned. She didn't have time for a shower. She got up, did a quick wash, struggling to find clothes she could wear to breakfast. She still didn't know where they would meet, but she hoped it would be close by.

When she was ready, she snatched her phone and checked it. Sure enough, Vince had texted her to meet them at a little coffee shop around the corner from the greenhouses. She sent back a note, saying she was leaving soon. Then she grabbed her purse and walked outside.

When she got into the little restaurant, she saw the men were already there. She walked over with a big smile. Vince hopped up and gave her a bone-crunching hug. When she could, she stepped back, stretched up and kissed him on the cheek. "You're still just a big boy, aren't you?"

He gave her a mock look of outrage but chuckled. "Too much, huh?"

She smiled and sat on the bench beside him. "You were *always* too much."

"Is that why you would never go out with me?" he complained.

She gave him a sideways look. "You never asked, for one," she said gently. "And I much preferred men, not boys." She delivered that last sting with a big smile.

He rolled his eyes at her and motioned for the waitress.

Raina turned to Reyes, who was sitting across the table, studying the two of them and their interaction. She leaned over, squeezed his fingers and said, "Good morning."

The corner of his mouth kicked up in a grin that made her heart melt.

"Good morning," he said. "You and Vince still act like school kids."

She shook her head. "I'm not. That's all Vince."

But Reyes just grinned at her. "It takes two to tango."

She rolled her eyes. "So how long are you staying?"

He shrugged. "Not very long. Maybe today, tomorrow, not sure."

She nodded. "I'm sure your dad is delighted to see you."

"He is indeed," Reyes said.

Just then the waitress arrived with hot coffee. She placed the cups on the table and handed out menus. After a crappy night like she'd had, Raina was hungry.

As she looked over the options, Reyes said, "Look at this. I haven't had coconut pancakes in a long time. That's what I'll have."

She stared at the pancakes option on her menu and wondered what the hell coconut pancakes were. She tended to be a plain foodie. Although she loved coconut, she wasn't sure about having it in her pancakes. She slowly lowered the menu, having picked out her choice, and placed her order with the waitress. When she left them, Raina glanced at the others. "Did anybody hear anything from my sister last night?"

The men both shook their heads. "We were going to ask you that question."

She shrugged. "There's been nothing on my phone. And there's no point in phoning her if she doesn't have hers with her."

"Any chance she has two phones?" Reyes asked.

"If she does, I don't know about it," Raina said honestly. "It would be nice if she'd get in touch with us soon though. I know my mom is pretty upset. I didn't call her yet this morning because I know she wouldn't have had much sleep, and I didn't want to wake her."

The waitress came back and delivered glasses of water. "I'll be back with your food shortly."

Vince looked over at Reyes. "So, what are you doing these days?"

Reyes straightened slightly and smiled. "The best kind of work," he said. "Similar to what we used to do in the navy but private jobs."

Vince leaned forward. "Do you think they're hiring?"

"I have no clue. But the boss is here, if you want to meet her."

"Maybe? Do I know anybody else working there?" Vince appeared to be interested but weary.

Raina glanced from one to the other. "I don't even understand what kind of work you do," she said. "I know you went into the navy, but I don't know what you did there either."

"We did a lot of stuff," Vince said. "Top-secret military ops that nobody ever knows about. It's one of the reasons I got out early."

"Why?" she asked. "Couldn't you keep a secret?"

He chuckled. "I keep secrets just fine," he said seriously. "But it's not always easy being in the middle of war-torn countries. After that last bout in Afghanistan, I walked. But I feel like, ever since, I've been trying to find the good things I had in the navy. That sense of camaraderie. Knowing you have a team, and you're part of something you can respect."

Reyes agreed. "That's what I have now. It still sometimes deals with war-torn countries, but it could also be doing things like escorting a movie star on a trip." He shrugged. "Or moving rare artifacts across the world. From day to day, absolutely no way to know what we'll be doing."

"But you're still dealing with countries?" Vince asked. His gaze narrowed. "That means you're a pretty big operation."

"We're not as big as the companies with defense contracts for other countries," Reyes said. "I'm not sure Levi and Ice want to get into that or to get that big. But we have men traveling around the world all the time. A group is in Africa right now with another company we work closely with. Bullard needed a bunch more men for a couple jobs, so four of us are over there."

Vince was surprised. "Now that's interesting." He leaned forward. "But let's be honest. What about the pay?"

At that, Reyes laughed. "Considering everything that's included, I'm doing way the hell better than I was in the service."

Raina listened with interest. It was a different world to

her, but she was so close to these men that she was glad for the insight. She hadn't understood why Vince had left the navy. At the time he just gave her a crooked grin and said something about needing a different mind-set, needing to see other things than just the negative.

Even now she didn't quite understand, but, if they were in war-torn countries, she couldn't imagine it was very nice. She'd known Vince had gone to Afghanistan, and that had to be brutal too. But it sounded like Reyes was really enjoying life with the new company.

"We live together on the business property, called the compound, or some live outside the compound in apartments Levi built on his land close by. They have completely furnished family apartments on the property, and the actual main building itself has dozens of bedrooms. We have Albert and Bailey who run the kitchen, so we have three gourmet meals a day, unlimited coffee and treats. There is a rec center, a gym, a medical center that's huge. Part of the reason why I'm here is the big pool. It's being worked on right now. They're tiling the inside, and Ice is trying to get the right plants to help create the look she wants."

Vince stared at him. "Pool, weight room, medic center? How big is this place?"

Reyes smirked. "I think she's up to twenty-two acres now, but the main compound itself is probably three or four acres. It's quite the place," he admitted. "We have two helicopters, and Ice is the pilot. She does a lot of the flights in and out as needed. Other than that, we fly out of the Houston airport."

Raina was fascinated that the woman at the center yesterday was a helicopter pilot. She didn't look like one. But she did have that no-nonsense, can-handle-anything look.

"Helicopters?" Vince asked, his tone low. "Seriously?"

Reyes leaned forward. "And that's nothing. You should see our armory."

She couldn't help but catch the grin on Vince's face and how his eyes lit up at Reyes's words. "Well, there you go. Now you got his attention," she muttered.

The men continued to talk. She listened, not part of the conversation. She pulled out her phone yet again and checked for a message from her sister, but there were none.

Her phone rang while she was holding it though. "Hi, Mom. I'm at a restaurant with friends," she said. "I haven't heard any updates from Reana."

"Neither have I," her mother said, her voice drawn and tired. "I'd hoped to sleep in this morning, but apparently I can't."

"I'll let you know as soon as I hear anything," Raina said. She hung up and placed the phone beside her knife and fork.

The food arrived slowly, with the coconut pancakes first. By the time she got her plate, the men were already digging in. But then she was eating about half the amount they were. She had a traditional waffle with a fried egg and sausage on the side.

As she finished her last bite, placing her knife and fork on her plate, she looked up to see two police officers walking into the coffee shop. They stood at the entrance, their gazes slowly moving across the patrons. When they landed at her table, her heart sank.

"Uh-oh," she said. "This doesn't look good."

Reyes looked at her with a frown. "What the devil do they want?" he muttered.

The men stacked their dirty plates to the side and

reached for their coffee, almost as a defense mechanism. When the officers arrived, they looked at the three of them.

The first one asked, "Which one of you is Reyes?"

"I am," Reyes said. "What can I do for you?"

Instead of answering him, they looked at Raina and asked, "Are you Raina Woodcroft?"

Slowly she nodded her head, her heart sinking even further. "What's this about?"

"We need to know where you were last night."

But they didn't direct it at anybody in particular. It seemed like the police wanted to know where each of them had been last night.

"I was at home alone," Raina said.

Reyes popped up next. "I was with my boss at her father's house." He rattled off the address.

"The whole night!"

Reyes frowned. "Yes, the whole night."

"Can anyone vouch for that?"

She watched a stillness cross his face. "Well, I was with both of them up until I went to bed, and that was about eleven o'clock. Then I got up this morning, had a quick cup of coffee with the two of them before Vince picked me up for breakfast."

"Did you sleep alone last night?"

He replaced the cup of coffee on the table in front of him, nodding slowly. "Yes, I did. But there is security at the house, and I'm sure it would record whoever was coming and going."

The two officers exchanged a look and continued to write on their notepads.

Reyes repeated, "What's going on?"

But they insisted on questioning Vince on his movements and then questioning Raina again.

Finally she couldn't stand it. "Is this about my sister?"

The officers turned their gazes on her. "What about your sister?"

"We can't find her," she said boldly. "I called her last night and left messages. She called me back, and it was a very strange conversation. Then in the next hour or hour and a half, I got a series of calls from her, but nobody was on the other end. Vince went and checked out her place for me, but she wasn't there. However, her phone was."

By now the officers were writing furiously.

She waited until the pens stopped moving and in a hard voice asked, "What's going on?"

The officers hesitated, and then one said, "We need the three of you to come to the station please."

She shook her head. "I'm due at work very soon."

Reyes, on the other hand, stood. "She's dead, isn't she?" he asked in a low voice. "It's the only reason you've been acting like this."

The officers studied him with fresh interest. "Did you have anything to do with her death?" one asked, his tone hard but low.

But Raina was stuck on Reyes's words. She reached out and grabbed the officer's arm. "Is my sister dead?" she whispered in a harsh, angry voice. "Are you telling me that my sister is dead?" Her voice rose. "Is Reana dead?" Pain, unimaginable pain ripped through her gut. She bent over, gasping for air.

Vince grabbed her hand. "Easy. We don't know that for sure."

But she looked at the officers and saw the answer in their eyes.

Reana was dead.

REYES'S STOMACH SANK. He knew he shouldn't have come back to California. Every time he was here, that damn woman caused him nothing but trouble. Immediately he felt sorry for his thoughts. It was the wrong thing to think and the wrong thing to feel. If Reana was dead, then it was devastating for her sister and her mom.

"What happened to her?" he asked, refusing to move. He still stood at the edge of the restaurant table.

He could see Raina shaking as she sat at the table. Vince still gripped her hand, trying to calm her down. It was a shitty way to find out your sister was dead. Notifying next of kin wasn't usually done interrogation style.

"I guess you guys don't get trained on how to inform family members of their deceased loved ones, do you?"

One of the officers winced, as if he realized how badly they'd misjudged the scenario. But the other one just glared at Reyes.

"When we pulled a list of people who most likely want her dead, you came at the top," he said. "Sorry. We want to discuss your whereabouts for last night."

"The only reason you would do that," he said, his voice hard, his gaze straight at the officer, "is if she didn't die of natural causes or of an accident."

"She was found dead in her car, murdered," the other officer said. "The vehicle was parked in the back of a large coffee shop parking lot."

Reyes brushed off the policemen and helped Raina stand on her feet. She wrapped her arms around him. He could do nothing but hold her close. He wanted to clap his hands over her ears and stop this conversation, but it was way too late for that. She trembled in his arms. He wanted to take her away from this ugliness, yet knew it would be so much worse soon.

When he could, he looked at the officers and asked, "How?"

But the first officer wasn't having any of it. "We'll talk at the station, and maybe then you can tell us."

He stiffened, but it was nothing compared to Raina's reaction.

She spun and said, "You can stop looking at him as a suspect. If anything happened to my sister, a hell of a lot of people didn't like her or had a grudge against her. You're not picking on Reyes. He just got into town."

"Convenient, isn't it?" Vince said. "He hasn't been here for two years, then somebody murders a woman the minute Reyes arrives."

"Looks like motive and opportunity to me," one officer said, his voice snide. "An ex-fiancé who doesn't like the way the woman he loves acts, then comes back and dishes up the revenge he'd planned for two years."

It was just too unbelievable. Reyes listened to them outline how he supposedly was angry because she'd broken up with him. And how he had plotted for two years and then took the opportunity to come back into town and kill her.

"Do you think I'm stupid?" he asked in a strangled voice. "I just arrived. It's pretty damn obvious if I came in and killed her right off the bat. I could have arranged for something from a distance, and you would never have connected me."

The other officer sent him an assessing gaze.

At that, Reyes said, "And who the hell did you ask? Who

would tell you that I was the one most likely to kill her?"

"We didn't have to ask anyone. She had a napkin in her hand that read Reyes."

He stared. "*Reyes*? My name? So, because she's got something against me, you're assuming she's talking to you, a future police officer who *might* be standing over her dead body?" Even to his ears that sounded more ludicrous than believable. "Maybe she wrote that because I'd know how to find her killer? Maybe she wrote that earlier as a reminder to call and to apologize me for her behavior?"

Both men appeared to take his point, but they shrugged.

"We are here to ask you what you know about her death."

"No, you aren't," Raina said, some of her defiance gone and just a weary sadness in her voice. "You came to accuse him." She glanced at Reyes. "Let's go downtown. We'll get all the details and then figure out what happened on our own," she snapped.

He looked down at her in surprise. But her gaze was hard and unflinching as she stared at him.

"You and I both know an awful lot of people didn't like her," she said in a low voice. "I love my sister, but I have no illusions about who she was."

He nodded, wrapped an arm around her shoulder and turned to look at Vince. "You coming?"

"Hell yes, I'm coming," he snapped. "But I think you need to tell your boss where you're going, and, if she has anybody who can help, she needs to pull them in."

At that, Raina gasped. "Damn. I'm late for work. I need to tell Annemarie I won't be in today." She pulled her phone from her pocket and stepped off to one side and called the garden center.

Reyes half listened to her conversation as she told his mother that she wouldn't be in until later. Annemarie didn't appear to be very happy about it, but then she had a very busy store right now, and anybody calling in sick or not making their shift would put her place under stress.

Then his phone rang. It was Ice. In a low voice he explained the problem.

Being typical Ice, she said, "Go to the police station with them. I'll meet you there." She hung up.

He smiled and pocketed the phone.

"Who did you just speak to?" one of the officers asked.

"My boss called me," Reyes said in a calm tone. "Ice. She and Levi own Legendary Security." When there was a flicker of awareness in the second officer's eye, Reyes nodded. "Yeah, I'm one of them. But that's all right. Take me down on a murder charge without even checking out any facts. That's smart."

"We didn't accuse you of anything," the second officer said. "And we certainly haven't charged you."

"Good, because we'll go through the questioning, and then you'll charge me or not. Either way I'll have the lawyers there in no time." He led the way toward the door. "Can Vince drive on his own, or do you want him in the back of the police car too?"

Both officers hesitated.

Then Vince said, "You're not being charged. We're all going to the station together." He reached out a hand for Raina and led her toward the door, then announced to anybody listening, which at this point was the entire restaurant, "I'm sorry for the bad news everyone, but Reana Woodcroft has been murdered. Of course these officers are trying to do their job, just not with any finesse."

There were gasps of shock because it was a small town. Both twins were well-known, as were all of Reyes's family.

One of the men in the back stood and said, "Well, you can bet this lot had nothing to do with it."

The officer looked at him. "Why is that?"

"Because they're family," he said. "All of them together. They've been a close family. They might have problems, but they sure don't need to kill each other."

The cops looked at each other, back at him again and said, "Unfortunately, when it comes to murder, it's almost always a friend or a family member who did the deed."

On that note, they pushed the three outside the restaurant.

"Hey, excuse me."

Hearing the waitress's voice, Reyes, at the last moment, remembered they hadn't paid the bill. He pulled out his wallet, grabbed money and handed it to the waitress. "Sorry," he said. "It was a great breakfast."

With the cop nudging him forward, they walked out. Knowing he was the prime suspect, he got in the back of the cruiser and told the other two, "Meet me there." He sat in the back seat of the police cruiser and buckled up. As the officers got in, he said, "You might want to watch your *P*s and *Q*s from here on in."

"Yeah? And why is that?" the first cop asked. "You some sort of royalty?"

"No," Reyes said. "But I'm an innocent man, one who doesn't take kindly to being treated like he's a criminal."

"You know what they say about innocence in this country? It's not that you're innocent until proven guilty now. You better prove you're innocent, or you're going down for a murder charge." And he turned on the engine and drove away.

# Chapter 6

RAINA SAT BESIDE Vince on the way to the police station. She was numb. The shock waves just kept hitting her. First, her sister was dead, and Raina couldn't get her mind wrapped around that. She was bombarded with images of her sister as a young girl, then as an older woman, and all the weird phone calls made from Reana last night. Second, all of that was overlaid with the thought that the police suspected Reyes of having had something to do with her demise.

Under her breath she muttered, "They have to be wrong."

"They *are* wrong," Vince reassured her. "At least the part about Reyes having anything to do with it. I'm so sorry for you though. It's a hell of a way to find out about your sister."

She shook her head. "I can't believe it. I need to see her and make sure it's her. I don't want my mother to find out from anyone else. I need to see Mom as soon as I can, but I need to know for sure that it's Reana—that there's no chance a mistake has been made."

"We might arrange that today," Vince said quietly. "Depends on the detectives and how they handle their investigations. Plus how long they wait until an autopsy is done. In cases of murder, an autopsy is generally done, unless particularly strong religious reasons may fight it. Even then I think the law trumps religion."

She stared at him and admitted softly, "I hadn't considered that. I don't know what to say to my mom about that. I feel like an autopsy would upset her. A violation of her daughter in a way."

He glanced at her before returning his gaze to the traffic. "You have to consider the cops may have already told her."

"Have they? I should be with her," she said in bewilderment. "We only heard ten minutes ago. She can't be alone after hearing something like that. She's never been terribly stable, as you know."

"I know. I'm so sorry. Let's hope they haven't notified next of kin yet or that the cops consider you as notified, and that's sufficient."

It would never be sufficient. Yet, knowing how devastated her mother would be, she realized she'd need to be there with her for most of the day. Hell, it could easily be for the next week. "We also have to tell Annemarie," she said. And then she turned to look at Vince. "Unless you think she already knows."

He shrugged. "I don't know if Reyes called her or not. I know he called his boss. I don't think he called his mother. But someone at the restaurant might have. This is really a small community when it comes to gossip."

She gave a broken laugh. "What kind of broken families are we from? The police tell the sister not the mother, and Reyes calls his boss and not his mother or father. You'd think his parents would be the most supportive in a case like this."

"Do you really think so?" Vince shook his head. "When you think about it, I'm not sure that's true. Reyes often had trouble with his mom. I know they love each other, but they weren't close like Ron and his mom were."

"No, because his mom was too much like Reana," she said. "I have to wonder if that's what the attraction was. They say sons marry women like their mothers."

"I've heard that. But, when you don't have a great relationship with your mother, you'd think you'd avoid that type."

"True, but I don't think Reyes thought about that in connection to his relationship with Reana. And, once he got caught up in her, I don't think he knew how to get out of it. Not until she broke up with him."

"Interesting." Vince's tone was suspiciously neutral. "I always figured you and he would be better together."

"There never was a *him and me*," she said. "Once Reana went after him, he fell—hook, line, and sinker."

"Until he woke up," Vince said calmly. "And then he got out."

"Did he though?" She shook her head, unsure what to believe anymore. "If you listen to the stories my sister told, he two-timed her with somebody else."

"That's *not* what happened," he said with certainty. "But I'm not the one to tell you about it. Trust Reyes. He's a good man."

She studied his profile. "You know him pretty well, don't you?"

Vince nodded. "We've been best buds for a long time," he said quietly. "I talked to him about Reana. I thought it was a destructive relationship and wanted him to get the hell away from her."

That was news to Raina. Not only that Vince had recognized how bad the relationship was but that he'd interfered. "I tried to do the same thing with my sister," she said sadly. "But she just laughed and said Reyes suited her purposes."

"And that's the problem," Vince said. "Everything had to suit Reana's purposes."

"Well, she manipulated the wrong person. God, I still can't believe it," she added in a hushed whisper.

"I know it's a little hard to think of somebody so vibrant and so passionate as now being gone."

"I want to see her," Raina said again. "I *have* to see her. I won't believe it otherwise."

They pulled into the police department's parking lot. Vince turned off the engine and focused on her. "Are you okay?"

She turned her gaze on him. "No, of course I'm not okay," she exclaimed. "My sister has been murdered. My whole world has been tossed upside down."

He nodded. "Well, let's go and find out what facts we can, take care of whatever we need to, and then let's get you home to your mom, so you can tell her, can be with her."

She slowly shook her head. "I'm not looking forward to that."

"First off, let's deal with what's in front of us." He opened the driver's door and walked around to the other side. She was still trying to get out. He held out his hand to her.

She placed hers in it and stood slowly. "They can't really believe Reyes had anything to do with this, can they?"

Vincent's face was grim when he said, "It depends on how much contact he's had with your sister over the last little while. Of course he looks good because of the fight they had at the greenhouses yesterday. Though who told the cops about it, I don't know."

"Did anyone?" she asked. "I figured it had more to do with Reana's note they found in her hand."

"I hate to say it because your sister is a bit of a bitch, but what if she did that on purpose?"

Raina's back stiffened. She hated to think anybody would even contemplate such a thing. And then she realized just how much her sister had come to hate Reyes, and Raina had to wonder. "That would only wash if she committed suicide," she said slowly. "I can't see her committing suicide."

"I agree. If she died in a fit of her bad temper, maybe. But most people who commit suicide don't destroy their own lives so they can destroy somebody else's. They usually find a way to destroy somebody else's life without touching theirs. So that goes back to maybe we need to make sure it really is your sister in the morgue."

"Right." She quickly picked up the pace. "That's the first thing I want to do."

"You have to be prepared for the fact they might not allow you to see her."

She shook her head. "I don't think any law will stop a family member from having a chance to confirm that the person they loved is dead."

"I don't know," Vince said. "When it comes to this stuff, the laws don't seem to make sense or to protect the families."

They walked inside the station to see Reyes sitting at the front desk, waiting. He looked up, saw them and smiled.

Raina rushed to his side, Vince right behind her. "I figured you'd be in an interrogation room or something."

"I would be, but Ice and the lawyers were here waiting for me. So that's been kiboshed," he said with a smirky grin. "I will be questioned. I'm just waiting for them to find a room we can use." He pointed at the empty chairs beside him. "Take a seat. It may be a while."

She looked around. "Where's your lawyer?"

He pointed behind him.

She saw a tall man in a business suit on the phone. Ice stood near him, also on the phone. Both looked serious but also had that we-mean-business attitude. Raina smiled, having a heartfelt rush of relief that Reyes had somebody to really support him. "I'm so happy they're here for you," she said warmly. "I know you had nothing to do with Reana's death."

"How can you know that?" His gaze was piercing. "You were there when she smacked me across the face yesterday."

Raina nodded. "Yes, I was. I have no clue what that was about. And, from the look on your face, neither did you. The trouble is, my sister was all about creating drama. And, in the last two years that you've been gone, I've barely even heard your name mentioned. I don't think she was pining for you. I think she was more concerned about you causing trouble when you came back, and she was trying to nip it in the bud—or at least to confuse the issue. But I don't know why."

He slowly nodded his head. "That could be."

She sat down beside him. "But why? What is it that you could do that would cause trouble for her?"

He hesitated, glanced at Vince for any thoughts, didn't get any, then faced Raina again.

She leaned forward and pressed further. "Tell me, please. It's well-past time for hiding any of this stuff. If that's really my sister who's been murdered, we'll need to know everything anyway."

He stretched out his legs, crossed his arms over his chest and leaned back. He studied her for a long moment before asking, "How much do you know about your sister's sex life?"

She wrinkled her face. "Not much. She talked lots about all kinds of things. Some I didn't want to hear. Such as, she often commented on how she picked fights with you because the makeups were so passionate."

He stared at her in surprise. "Is that what she said?"

Raina nodded. "She used to call me an icicle and *frozen* and *cold* because I didn't have her same passionate temperament," she admitted. "I'm just much more reserved and calm. And I don't really want to have my private life publicized the way she wanted to do with hers."

He stared across the lobby. "How much do you know about why we broke up?"

"Not a clue," she said. "She told me that she found you in bed with another woman."

"That's what she told Ron too," he said slowly. "But that's not true."

Vince nodded, his expression grim.

"I figured it wasn't because that isn't who you are," Raina said to Reyes.

His lips quirked. "Thanks for the vote of confidence."

She shrugged. "I knew you a lot better than she did. We've been friends since forever, but she wasn't part of our friend group."

He nodded, saw Vince nodding too, then seemed to make a sudden decision. "The reason we broke up was because I went to her place one day and found her in bed with someone else." His voice was low. "And it wasn't a guy. She was in bed with another woman. And it was obvious what they were doing."

Raina sat back and stared at him. "What?"

He nodded slowly. "We had words before I walked

away. But she got busy telling everybody, to save face, that I was the one who had an affair, not her."

Raina sagged back in the chair, her mind in complete chaos as she tried to fit that puzzle piece into what she knew about her sister. And it just didn't work. "Are you sure it was Reana?"

He nodded. "Absolutely. It was at her brownstone. We spoke at the time, but I've not spoken to her since then. The first I saw her in two years was when she came into the store yesterday and smacked me across the face. I figured she must be worried I might say something and ruin her reputation." He shrugged. "I'm totally okay if she was a lesbian, but I wanted honesty from her in terms of our own relationship because, if that's where she was leaning, then she didn't belong with me. And something was definitely wrong in our relationship."

It was too much for Raina. She studied him, looking for any signs of lies or deceit, but there were none. "I don't know what to say. That's the last thing I would have thought anybody would have said about my sister. I know she was into experimentation but hadn't expected that."

"Like you just said, her sexuality was open," Vince interrupted her musings. "Maybe she was trying that one before she got married, or that was a secret part of her life she didn't want anybody to know about."

"She definitely needed to try anything and everything before it was too late," Raina said.

"This wasn't the first time for them," Reyes said. "The other woman was crying and telling Reana how she needed to confess, to tell the truth about her feelings. We had quite the blowup. Then I just walked. It's taken me a long time to realize, as I look back on the relationship, the little signs I hadn't seen. Once I realized what was going on, it made sense to me. But, for whatever reason, your sister wasn't prepared to acknowledge where her sexuality lay. And potentially she was happy with either sex. But she loved that woman. She didn't love me."

Raina swallowed hard. "I guess the next answer I need to know is …" She searched his handsome face. "Who was that other woman?"

HE SHOULD HAVE realized that would be the question uppermost in everyone's minds. The trouble was, he didn't know. "I'd never seen her before," Reyes said. "And her name wasn't mentioned in the short discussion we all had."

"Of course not," Vince said. "That would be way too easy. Because anybody else in this lovely sordid love triangle will look good for murder. We need to find the other woman."

Reyes nodded. "I guess I never contemplated that she might be involved in the murder. I don't know if your sister was still together with her or not."

"I can't say," Raina said, "because I didn't know about her in the first place."

"What did she look like?" Vince asked.

"She was in bed, mostly nude, that's what I saw." Reyes's tone was short. "Her hair was long, brunette, wavy. She was a classic beauty, long aquiline nose, high cheekbones." He paused, thinking about it. "Honestly, outside of trying to figure out what the hell was going on, she wasn't the focus of my attention. It was my fiancée in bed with her. That's where my attention was," he said.

"Understandable," Raina said. "But that description

doesn't ring a bell. I can't place a woman like that."

"Have you seen her since?" Vince asked.

"No," Reyes said. "I hadn't seen her before. I didn't recognize her, and I haven't seen her since. But it's not like I stuck around."

Silence fell on the three of them as they waited for the cops to come. When they did, all three of them were taken to separate interview rooms.

Reyes walked into the small room to find his lawyer right behind him. He smiled and said, "I know it's a job to you, but I really didn't have anything to do with this."

The lawyer nodded. "I believe you. I've also known Ice for a long time, and she believes you. It's good enough for me. Now let's get this over with."

They took their seats, and the two detectives who had accosted them at the restaurant came in. Reyes answered all their questions, but they didn't ask anything more than what he'd already answered at the restaurant.

"I understand you had an ugly breakup with the deceased?" This officer's name was Jacob Laudner.

Answering Detective Laudner's question, Reyes said, "Depends on what you mean by ugly. I found her in bed with another woman, yes."

At that, the two officers lifted their heads from writing their notes.

He nodded. "Yes, you heard me. She was in bed with another woman."

"According to two of her coworkers and your own mother, you had an affair, and she found you out."

"That's the story Reana told everyone. She had to save face as to why we broke up, and I had left town, so she was free to say whatever the hell she wanted."

"We've already spoken to your mother, and your mother backs up Reana's story."

"That's nice," Reyes said steadily. "My mother and Reana are good friends My mother would probably believe anything Reana said to her. The truth of the matter is, it was all lies. But then that's what Reana did well."

Detective Laudner settled back in his chair. "So you're saying something completely different than what everyone else is saying about Reana?"

Reyes knew he was on difficult ground. "I don't know about that. Reana was one of those people who only let a certain number of people see who she really was. She was all about appearances."

The other detective, Detective Burgess, asked, "Can anybody collaborate?"

"Collaborate what? That she was having an affair? Well, that would be the other woman in bed, but, no, I don't know who she is. I'd never seen her before that night, and I haven't seen her since."

Detective Burgess studied Reyes's face for a long moment. "So you're creating a fictional character to confuse the issue."

Suddenly tired of the whole thing, realizing this was just the tip of the iceberg, Reyes said, "Hardly. I'm sure, if you contact the security company for Reana's apartment building, you'd see this woman coming and going. For all I know, she lived there with her."

"That must have made you angry, to have found her in bed with another woman."

"So you're saying that, two years ago, I was really angry. I left for all that time, and, in the meantime, I plotted her death?" Reyes asked in astonishment. "I come back to town with my boss to my family's company, and I kill her the first night I arrive?"

"Did you?"

Reyes rubbed his temple, trying to marshal his thoughts. "I did not kill Reana. I saw her for five minutes at the store yesterday, and that's it. You've already asked me about a time line for my whereabouts last night, and I gave it to you."

"For all I know, you slipped out of the house, killed her and sneaked back in with both your host and your boss as your witnesses."

He stared at them in surprise. "Wow, that's an awful lot of effort for somebody in bed with another woman two years ago."

"She was your fiancée. She duped you. Not only having an affair but with a woman. How does a man compete with that?"

"He doesn't." Reyes shook his head. "The thing is, I went there to break up with her. So finding her in bed was just an easy way out. It was a great save on my part. What could have been an ugly scene was an ugly scene but for a whole different reason." His tone had turned hard. "I walked out with a sense of relief that I had a clear conscience, and I hadn't had to hurt her."

"So now you're saying you went there to break up with her."

"I would have said it earlier, but I didn't get a chance. All you wanted to know about was why we broke up. The reason was, I found her in bed, but it would have happened anyway," he said. "I went there to break up with her."

"And why were you breaking up with her?"

"Because it was like living in a soapbox. It didn't matter what the issue was, there was drama, there were fights, there was turmoil nonstop."

The officers asked him several more questions, but he had no other information. He hadn't had any contact with her, hadn't had any phone calls with her, hadn't seen her in the ensuing years. "And, no, I haven't seen her sister or her mother in all that time either. Hell, I haven't seen my own brother and my parents in the past two years either."

"And what about the woman you say you saw in bed with her? Can you give us a description?"

He nodded and gave the same description he'd given Raina. "Somebody has to know about her," he said heavily. "And, for all we know, she's the one who may have killed Reana."

"Bloody convenient," Detective Burgess said.

"Not very," Reyes said. "I came here for a couple days to see my family and to help my boss. Other than that, I wouldn't have come at all."

Detective Laudner stood up. "The interview is over for the moment. But don't leave town."

Reyes stared at him. "Are you serious? I have to go back to Texas, back to work."

"You don't get to leave town until we say so," Detective Burgess said. "And I don't care how much pull your boss has. Or your lawyer, for that matter."

Reyes turned to look at his lawyer, who was busy writing down notes.

The lawyer stood and said, "We'll see about that. As far as hassling my client goes, you're done with that too."

"We didn't hassle him," Detective Burgess said. "All we did was interview him."

"The interview has ended," the lawyer said with a hard smile. "We'll discuss the rest as you try to do an investigation."

Reyes stood. "Do I get to know anything about what happened to Reana?"

"You probably already know," Detective Burgess said. "Why don't you tell us?"

Reyes opened his mouth to argue, but the detectives walked out. He turned to look at his lawyer and asked, "Can they do that? I don't even know how she died. For all I know it was a suicide."

"She was beaten up and shot," the lawyer said. "The autopsy is underway right now. And that's unusual in itself. Normally it takes a couple days. It's a busy morgue. The coroners are beyond busy with multiple fatalities in this city. But someone pulled strings to give Reana priority. We have to wait for the results."

Reyes nodded thinking he likely had Ice to thank for the speediness of the autopsy. "I'd like to know as soon as anybody else does," he said. "Because I'm pretty sure Ice and her team will want to investigate this."

"They may want to," the lawyer said, "but the best thing for you is to keep your hands out of it."

Reyes gave him a hard look. "And, if you were in my position, would you?"

The lawyer gave a bark of a laugh. "Hell no. I'd be making damn sure I sorted this out because I couldn't trust the police. Sometimes they're good, and sometimes they're just damn sloppy. If they can find a way to nail this on your head, they wouldn't bother searching for another one. To them, you're looking like a very nice suspect, and they aren't putting in too much effort to find anybody else."

Reyes nodded. "That's what I mean. I need to know everything they know and investigate this myself."

"What you need to do," the lawyer said, "is find the woman's lover. Doesn't mean they still have to be involved the last two years, but, as soon as you can confirm what you saw, it'll shake things up a bit. It doesn't take your neck out of the noose, but it does throw in other likely suspects."

"The woman was bawling her eyes out back then," Reyes said as they walked through the hallway. "And she was devastated at Reana's anger at seeing me. I think, more than that, Reana wouldn't publicly acknowledge what they had between them. It was a secret, and that meant it was under the table, something she was ashamed of. The other woman wanted Reana to be honest and to confess her love, but she wouldn't do it."

"It sounds like Reana might not have loved her any more than she loved you. Did you consider that?"

Reyes stopped and thought about it, then said, "You're right. I can't know for sure that she did. The bottom line is, I don't think Reana loved anybody but Reana."

# Chapter 7

RAINA MAY HAVE thought being at the police station was hard, but standing over her dead sister's body had to be one of the worst moments of her life. She'd waited until she could see her sister, not wanting there to be any mistake before she spoke to her mother. Yet standing outside her mother's front door, she knew the worst was yet to come.

She had refused to let the guys come with her. They'd wanted to give her silent support, but she knew nobody could help her through this next hour.

She knocked on the door, but there was no answer. She knocked again, then pulled out her phone and called her mother. When there was still no answer, she stood, wondering what to do. She had a key to the house, but her mother was one of those who didn't take kindly to anyone accessing her private space. Like her sister.

Raina sat down on the front steps. A brick wall enclosed the house all the way around, except for the four porch steps that went down to the sidewalk. There she tried again to call. And got no answer. She couldn't help but panic at the thought of what was going on. Had her mother already learned about Reana's fate? That would explain why Mom was completely unavailable. But it also didn't say much about what her mother might be doing.

Raina pulled out her keys, unlocked the front door and

stepped in. "Mom? Are you home?"

No answer.

She called out again and again as she raced through the lower floor. No sign of her. Hitting the stairs to go up two at a time, she ran to the master bedroom. The door was shut. Hating to know what was on the other side, but knowing she had no choice, she knocked on the door hard. Still no answer. She opened the door and stepped in.

Her mother lay across the bed, her body lifeless. Raina moved to her mother's side, checking for a pulse on her neck. There was one, but it was incredibly faint. She grabbed her phone and called 9-1-1 as she tried to rouse her mother.

"Mom! Mom, wake up. Wake up."

But there was no response. Her mother's body flopped limply on the bed. The 9-1-1 call went through immediately, but Raina had to answer so many damn questions.

The dispatcher said, "We've already dispatched some-body to that address. I do need to get more information from you."

Raina sagged on the bed beside her mother. "Just hurry, please."

The woman continued to ask her questions: who she was, what her relationship was with the other woman, and what her home address was. By the time she was done, she could hear sirens coming up the street. "They're here. They're here," she said and hung up the phone.

She raced down the stairs and opened the door as the ambulance came to a stop. She called out before the first paramedic reached her. "She's upstairs in the main bedroom. She's unconscious. I don't know what's wrong."

The two men rushed past her, heading to her mother's side. She stood at the front door, hating the thought that her mother might have tried to commit suicide. She'd never been suicidal, as far as Raina knew, but it was the first thought that had crossed her mind. Somebody might have told her about Reana. And, if that was the case, Raina could definitely see her mother taking steps to stay close to her favorite daughter.

Raina didn't begrudge them their relationship—or rather she tried not to. She'd been happy for the two of them, but that hadn't minimized the hurt Raina felt.

Her mother had understood her sister more than Raina ever could. And that had just been so wrong. She and Reana were twins. They should have understood each other. She thought twins were supposed to finish each other's sentences, to understood everything about how the other one operated. But somewhere along early childhood, they'd taken divergent paths and had ended up so vastly different that they might as well have been strangers, speaking different languages.

Raina slowly walked upstairs and into the bedroom, watching the men work on her mother. Her hand went across her mouth instinctively, wrapping her arm around her stomach as she leaned against the wall out of the way.

One of the men asked her, "Do you know what happened?"

"No. I just got here a few minutes ago," she said. "I came by the house and found her like this."

"Is there a reason why she would have tried to commit suicide?"

Her voice broke as she said, "We just found out that my twin sister was murdered sometime in the last twelve hours."

Both of the men stopped.

She shrugged, tears coming to the corner of her eyes. "I only found out at about eight this morning. I came here to break the news to her. I just came back from the police station, confirming it was my sister's body." She swallowed hard, wiping at her eyes. "And this is how I found Mom."

"So I presume somebody else told her?"

"I don't know," she said in a broken whisper.

Her mother was quickly strapped onto a gurney and wheeled out. They carried her down the stairs and put her in the ambulance.

"Do you know for certain that she tried to commit suicide?" she asked one of the men but only got a shrug.

Two police officers walked in at that moment. They did a quick search of her mother's bedroom and the adjoining bathroom. They came out with several pill bottles; all were empty.

She clapped a hand over her mouth as she stared at the empty bottles. She shook her head. "I don't even know where those are from," she said. "As far as I know, she wasn't on any medications."

And yet, the bottles had her mother's name on them. A sob broke free, and Raina didn't know what to do anymore. She sank down on a chair beside the bed as the police continued to search.

"There wasn't a letter though?" one of the officers asked. "What's going on?"

"Maybe you should check with the two detectives I spent an hour with today. My sister was murdered sometime during the night," she said, sobbing. "I'm sorry. I'm sorry. I just can't answer any more questions right now."

And suddenly she wasn't alone anymore. Reyes sat beside her, his arms wrapped around her waist as he picked her up and sat her on his lap. He just held her close.

He told the police officers, "You'll have to talk to Detectives Laudner and Burgess. We just came from the station, answering their questions. Apparently her sister was beaten and shot sometime during the night. Raina's already traumatized from that. Finding her mother like this, she needs more time."

The officers nodded in compassion. "There isn't a suicide note, so we have to treat this as suspicious. Can you tell me if she had any suicidal tendencies? Was she dealing with any depression or any major trauma, financial ruin, a breakup, anything?"

Raina shook her head. "No, no, no. I think it has to be related to my sister's murder, but I don't know for sure."

The officer nodded and proceeded to talk to a photographer who had suddenly arrived.

Reyes picked her up, carried her down the hallway into the closest bedroom of the three upstairs, a small room where he laid her on the bed and sat beside her. He pulled the bedcovers over her and said, "Just lie here and rest."

She stared up at him, her eyes huge wells of pain. "What the hell is going on?"

He gripped her fingers. "You know very well that your mother might have tried to commit suicide if she knew about Reana. They were very close."

Raina nodded. "That's what I suspected when I saw her. But I didn't tell her yet. I didn't have a chance to," she cried out.

"I know. That doesn't mean somebody else didn't."

She tried to think of who would have said something. Her mother did have a lot of friends, and so did Reana. It was quite possible somebody talked to her mom before Raina got here.

"Could have even been the police, I suppose," she said

sadly. "Poor Mom."

"Poor Mom, poor Reana and poor Raina," Reyes said quietly. "This will be a very difficult time for you."

She nodded slowly. "But I didn't have the relationship with Reana that Mom did."

"That doesn't mean you won't miss the connection you did have with your sister. She might not have been the easiest person to get along with, but you did love her. I have no doubt about that."

She smiled tremulously up at him. "I did," she whispered. "But it's a love that sometimes hurt. I kept trying to not compare myself to her, but it was hard. She was larger-than-life. It's like she was 150 percent, and I was only 50 percent."

He squeezed her fingers and shook his head. "Just because you were the quiet one, just because you were happy to be in the background, that doesn't mean you weren't as important or as nice or as stunning or as smart as she was. She was just one of those who always had to be in the limelight."

Raina knew he was trying to make her feel better, but nobody could tell her anything about her sister that she didn't already know. Her sister did have a lot of good qualities. And she would be sadly missed.

"I have to take care of funeral arrangements," Raina whispered. She wiped her eyes and tried to sit up, but he pushed her shoulders gently back down.

"You don't have to do that right now," he said. "If anything, I think you need to go to the hospital for your mother."

She pressed her eyes closed. "I should already have gone," she cried out.

"You couldn't have because I was holding you back. And you're not driving now either. I'll take you there myself."

She looked up at him with questioning eyes.

He leaned down and held her close. "You'll be okay," he said.

She shook her head. "I'm not so sure about that. It's like my whole world has been ripped apart."

"Murder will do that," he said, his tone serious. "Death is hard enough, but, when it comes in this form, it can mess up your mind. We don't know who is responsible or why, but we have to make sure whatever this is, it stops here. Your mother is already a casualty. Let's not have you collapse over it too."

Raina wasn't the kind to collapse. She was the kind who would get on with work, and months and weeks down the road she would finally break down and cry for days. But, right now, it was all bottled up inside while she carried on.

"I need to tell your mother."

"I will," he said with firm authority. He pulled out his phone, dialed his mother's number, and, when she answered, he said, "I don't know if you've been given an update yet, but Raina won't be in for the rest of today, maybe not for a couple days."

She could hear Annemarie's disapproving exclamation on the other end.

Reyes said, "Reana was murdered during the night, and Melissa has collapsed. She's been hospitalized. Raina is devastated obviously, but is holding it together."

And again Annemarie's voice, loud and full of shock, filtered through the phone line. Raina barely heard the words but enough to understand that the restaurant patrons who'd been there at breakfast had already spread the word.

Then something about the police.

Raina frowned. Of course the police had spoken to her mother. The detectives had relayed part of that conversation. It made Raina feel odd to hear everyone discussing her life. And Reyes's life. This had to be devastating to him. To hear the suspicion in people's voices, to know they questioned if he'd been involved. … She loved her sister, but having that napkin in her hand at the end …

"We don't have all the details on Reana's death yet," Reyes said. "Because she smacked me yesterday and because of the fact she was found with my name written on a napkin, apparently the police consider me the prime suspect."

Dead silence followed on the other end of the phone, and then Annemarie exploded with the same passionate outrage Raina would have expected. She smiled to hear her defense of her son. And it made Raina feel better. Reyes had the worst part of the deal.

When he finally got off the phone, she smiled up at him. "Your mother is so much like my sister."

He nodded. "Yes, and, as my father has repeatedly said, it takes a great deal of patience and tolerance to live with her. He was surprised when I hooked up with your sister because she's so much like my mother. And I guess that's also why I wasn't surprised when I came to the realization I couldn't go through with that relationship. Ron is very much like my mother and deals with her well, whereas I'm much more like my father. I'm tolerant and silent in the background."

"As long as you don't let yourself get run over," Raina said quietly. "That was my problem. Reana was just bigger than any life force. She was a roller coaster to live with. It was a case of *get on board or get run over*."

"And then you ended up learning to dodge her and to

get out of her way instead," he said shrewdly. "It took me a little longer to figure that out, but, once I did, I knew I had to step out of her path and stay out of her path."

He reached over and gently stroked her cheek. "I should have stayed with you."

"You never were *with* me, not the way you were with her," Raina said sadly. "We might have gotten there, but, once my sister saw you in that light, and you saw my sister that way, … well …" She shrugged. "The rest is history." She could feel the intensity of his gaze. This gentle investigation of their feelings had her scared to say too much, and yet, scared not to say enough …

"I wonder if you can ever understand what that was like," he said. "I really wanted to get to know you better, but then I saw your sister again, … and I don't know what happened. … I didn't realize what taking that turn in my life would mean."

At least he said it with a note of humor, as if, looking back on his relationship with Reana, he didn't begrudge the time that he'd spent with her. Neither did he sound regretful for those "lost" years. Something else she appreciated now that Reana was dead. Maybe not so much had she still been alive …

"She really slept with another woman?" Raina studied his face intently. "That's the one thing I can't get out of my head. And yet, it's one more thing in a long line of craziness that I don't understand. How does any of this work together? It's like I didn't even know my sister."

"I think it's quite possible your sister has always had that sexual preference but couldn't accept it. Like it threatened her image of herself or how other people would view her. It's accepted more now, but I think it takes the right person and the self-confidence to stand up and to proclaim, *This is who I am*, and your sister didn't have that yet. It did make a lot of sense to me when I saw them together. All these little troubling aspects to our relationship never made sense before. *But*, when I saw them in bed together, the tumblers went *click*, and I finally understood. For all her exuberance and liveliness out of bed, she wasn't the same in bed."

Raina stilled. "Are you serious? She used to mock me because I was … What did she say? … *Vanilla* sex-wise."

"If you consider she was involved in a lesbian relationship, then that would make sense too." He studied her and then looked out the window. "Maybe she was fishing. Maybe she was wondering if her twin sister also had the same bent?"

"I have no clue," Raina said. "I've never felt the inclination to do so. I like men," she said with a smile, "and it seemed to me that my sister adored them."

"I think she adored what they could do for her as far as society and a lifestyle. But I think women fulfilled Reana on the inside," Reyes said sadly. "But she couldn't accept it or wasn't ready to go public with it, thus she cheated herself and her girlfriend out of what could have been a real relationship."

"And you," Raina said with a half smile.

Just then one of the police officers stepped in the doorway. "We're leaving now. We do need to ask you some questions before we go though."

Raina struggled to sit up. She leaned against the headboard, pulling the covers to her chest. "If you don't mind, let's do it now then," she said. "I'll head to the hospital in a few minutes and see my mother."

They went over her movements for the last twenty-four hours. After she was done, the officer asked Reyes the same questions. When he answered the last one, the officers said they would talk with the other two detectives about this and see if the cases could be worked jointly.

"Is there any chance my mother wasn't given a choice to take these medications?"

The police officer looked at her in surprise. "You mean, somebody might have forced her to take the pills so it would look like she tried to commit suicide?"

Raina nodded slowly. "I know I'm grasping at straws, but it's a little hard to understand her behavior."

"What was her relationship with you like?"

"Big sister," she said instantly. "Meaning, I was the big sister to my mom."

The officer studied her. "That's an interesting description."

She shrugged. "My sister and my mother were volatile. My mother seemed incapable of handling my sister and used to call me, asking how to handle Reana and what to do about her. For me it was more a case of live and let live and stay out of the way. But, of course, my mother couldn't accept that. And she wanted me to fix things all the time. She couldn't fix them, so she always called on me to do so. But I wasn't any good at fixing them because, honestly, my sister didn't want to fix anything."

The officer nodded slowly. "Here's my card." He pulled one out of his pocket and handed it to Reyes. "If you think of anything else, or you see anything untoward, anything missing from the house ... We don't think any foul play was involved, but, if something hits you wrong, then call me and let me know." He turned and walked out.

Raina swung her legs over the side of the bed and stood. "This has been a day I would like to have over with." She walked into the small bathroom and washed her face.

"Do you want me to take a look at your mom's room? See if anything is missing?"

She looked at him. "You've never been in there before today, have you? How would you know if anything was wrong?"

He gave her a crooked smile. "I wouldn't, but, if I was a detective working on the case, I wouldn't have seen Melissa's room before either."

She nodded. "Then please do."

She shut the bathroom door, used the facilities and washed her hands. She opened the door and stepped out of the bedroom and into the hallway to find him studying the layout of the house. "Did you find anything?"

"Did your mom sleep with the window or the balcony doors open?"

"Never," Raina said. "She always complained about drafts."

"The bedroom window is totally open," he said. "That struck me as odd for a woman living alone."

She frowned at him, rushed into her mother's bedroom. Not only was the big window open, so were the glass French doors to the balcony. "She never used the glass doors because outside stairs were connected to them. She always kept these doors bolted on the bottom, so nobody could get in."

"Was she nervous living here alone?"

Raina raised both hands, palms up. "Why ask me? Apparently I don't know anything about my family anymore. As far as I'm aware, she wasn't nervous, but she didn't like the idea of anybody coming into her bedroom, day or night. So she kept both the window and the balcony doors locked and bolted. She never went out there, never used that little balcony. At least not that I'm aware of."

He nodded and stepped out on the balcony, studying the layout of the backyard.

She joined him. "But I suppose it's easy for somebody to have gotten into her room, isn't it?"

"Or to have left this way, yes."

"And what about fingerprints? Wouldn't they have left fingerprints on the door latch?"

"It's possible," he said. "But then we have to assume he—or she—was an amateur."

Raina froze, then turned slowly to stare at him. "You're not thinking my sister's killer had something to do with my mother's attempted suicide, are you?"

He sighed. "I'm not suggesting anything," he said. "We have to assume nothing at this point. But, considering your mother and her mental state right now—if she already knew about your sister's murder—suicide would make sense in response to that. However, what if she and your sister had a major fight? Would she have still committed suicide?"

"I don't think so," Raina said. "They fought all the time. Besides she's the one who asked me to get in touch with my sister last evening. When I finally did, I contacted Mom and told her that Reana was fine."

"Maybe Reana came over to talk to her. What if Reana had told your mom that she was a lesbian. How would your mother have reacted?"

At that, her heart beat heavily, and her stomach sank. "My mother would not have accepted that," Raina said slowly. "Mom was against many things in life, and lots of them didn't really matter to her, but that one did. She said there was no reason for lesbians to exist, that something was wrong with them. She felt, if they could get the proper counseling, they would go straight."

"So, if your sister didn't dare tell your mother before, but then, for whatever reason, she decided to come clean ..."

"It would have been one hell of a fight," Raina said. "And I'm not sure who would have won that one."

"Reana would have," Reyes said. "I have no doubt."

"I don't know, but I highly doubt my mother would have turned around and committed suicide over it. But she definitely would have wanted to kill Reana." She listened to the words as they came out of her mouth and shook her head. "No, no, no, no. I didn't mean that. No way would Mom have killed Reana."

But it was already too late. Reyes leaned against the glass doors, his arms crossed over his chest. "But would she have?"

Raina swallowed hard. "You're thinking she might have killed my sister and then tried to commit suicide?" She started to hyperventilate. It was so damn hard to make her chest move to get air into her lungs again, and suddenly she found herself bent over double with Reyes pounding on her back. Finally she took several gulping breaths and collapsed onto the small balcony floor.

"Don't say things like that," she cried out. "Enough is going through my head without you putting more disturbing ideas in there."

"I didn't put the thoughts in there," he said. "You did."

She stared at him and bit down hard on her lip. She shook her head. "I would hope my mother would not have killed my sister. And I would hope that, if she had done something like that, she wouldn't have tried to commit suicide. But, when you lay it out like that, it is definitely possible. It's not very feasible, but it is possible," she admitted. "And now I feel like I'll be sick."

She bolted inside her mother's bathroom, where she opened the toilet just in time for her stomach contents to empty. She sat on the floor at the base of the toilet for a few minutes, waiting for the heaving to stop, and then Reyes handed her a glass of water. She rinsed her mouth and spat it out, flushed the toilet, slowly made her way to her feet and back out to the bedroom.

She thought about her mother lying there and the empty pill bottles on the bathroom counter, and she shook her head. "That doesn't explain why the doors and window are open. She would never have left them open."

"I know," he said. "We don't have any answers, no matter all the questions. I'm just throwing out ideas."

She lifted her straying gaze to his. "Then please come up with other ideas. I don't think I can handle these. To find out my sister has been murdered and then to think my mother could be the perpetrator? If she comes to, and that's what she says to me, I don't know how I'll live with it."

"You'll live with it the same way you always live with everything," he said. "With kindness and grace, being as understanding as you can be. Because obviously it would have taken an awful lot for your mother to have taken that step. And we don't know that she did. So let's keep an open mind, and we'll try to find the *right* answers, not just any answer." He walked toward her, wrapped her up in his arms and held her close.

HE HADN'T THOUGHT to have this opportunity to hold her so close, but her world had blown apart, and he couldn't do any less. She'd been an important part of his life at one time. She'd always been in his thoughts, even when he'd been away.

But he'd always wondered. Then he'd gotten into Reana's web, and he'd been lost, trying to figure a way out. Raina had been no help as she'd turned her back on him— something he could understand if she'd liked him and had been upset that he was going out with her sister. At the time she didn't seem to like him so much, and the more she'd turned away, the deeper into Reana's clutches he went, happy to have someone appreciate him. As he thought about it now, it made him realize just how young he'd been. But he was gone much of the time with his naval ops, and then it was easy to forget and dismiss all that was wrong in his relationship with Reana.

It had never occurred to him that she'd been unfaithful while he was off on missions, until he'd made that fateful decision to break up with her.

And what a nightmare that had been.

But he'd grown from that, like he had from so many turning points in his life, and he felt like he'd finally come full circle …

With the right woman at the right time.

And wasn't that something? He wanted to jump for joy and to tell Raina all about his new revelation, but she was buried against his chest and needed his comfort, not his declaration.

She also needed him to be there for her.

And that he could do. In fact, there was no place he'd rather be.

"We need to go," she whispered, stirring in his arms. "She needs me."

He did too, but that was for later. Much later.

He tilted her chin, dropped a kiss on her nose, as if it were the most natural thing in the world, and whispered, "Come on. I'll take you."

# Chapter 8

R AINA WAS BESIDE herself when she finally got to the hospital emergency room. For some reason the reaction over her mother's condition hit her hard as she walked in the entrance—as if finally realizing that, while Raina had been sorting through her own emotions, her mother may have passed away.

As soon as Raina could, she found somebody to ask about her mother's condition. Raina was redirected to doors to the emergency area, to one of the women standing at the counter. When she repeated her question, the woman smiled.

"She'll be all right. Her stomach is being pumped right now, and she's getting the treatment she needs. Please sit and wait. We'll give you an update as soon as we have one."

And that was the best she could get. Raina sat down in the emergency waiting area, Reyes beside her. She looked at him and said, "You don't need to stay. You should be off finding out who the hell did this. I'll stay here and wait for my mom."

He linked his fingers with hers, but his facial expression said something was on his mind.

She squeezed his fingers and whispered, "I know what you're thinking, and I don't want to believe it. But, if it's true, we need to find proof. What I don't want to do is go through life wondering what happened. So I give you full permission to go through any of my mom's personal belongings that you need access to. Surely, between you and Vince, somebody can figure out what the hell is going on." His gaze searched hers, and she smiled a little tremulously but was more emboldened now that she was here and had heard her mom would be okay. "Please do whatever you can."

He nodded, leaned forward and kissed her gently on the temple. "I will." Stepping back, he turned and said, "I have to also see my mother and talk to the staff. I don't know when anybody last saw your sister."

"You might as well check out her place too. I'll give you the keys to her place and mine," Raina said, the fatigue evident in her voice. She couldn't believe she'd come so close to losing the rest of her family. She fished out her spare keys. "I'm the only one left to help my mother, so please do what you can for her as well."

He nodded. "Give me any updates as they come through."

She smiled. "I will."

"And I'll be back in a couple hours. You'll need to eat."

She shook her head. "Right now I don't think I can get any food down."

"Probably not but you can't stay here either. Your mom will need a lot of rest and recovery, and there's no benefit to you staying here, not getting any sleep or food yourself." With that he left.

She sank into the hard, uncomfortable waiting room seat, her mind completely overwhelmed with everything she'd learned so far this day. The worst and most-destructive suggestion was that her mother might have killed her sister and then tried to kill herself. Raina didn't want any proof of such an awful suggestion, but, in the back of her mind, she couldn't help but wonder. Her mother had a temper; her sister had a horrible temper. When the two of them were on the wrong side of each other, it was pretty ugly to watch. Yet, even though they fought, they'd loved each other dearly.

What Raina didn't see was her mother trying to hide or to clean up a crime scene. Nor did she own a gun—at least not as far as Raina knew. But, as had been proven today, she didn't know all that much about her family, apparently.

So they needed to find out where her sister had been killed, then see if her mother had had a hand in it. If she didn't, what was her reason for trying to commit suicide? Though there was no proof of that attempt—certainly no suicide note—Raina didn't see any other way for her mother to have voluntarily inhaled a bellyful of pills. Yes, her mother had dealt with depression, but that had been years ago. Plus she had ongoing frustrations in her work and her life, and she certainly didn't like that she had no partner and hadn't had one in quite a while. Yet she wasn't currently depressed. At least not clinically.

Her mother also worried both her daughters were heading off to lives of their own. But her mother was never suicidal—again, as far as Raina knew. So surely even Reana's death was not reason enough for a suicide attempt right now for a mother with another daughter and for a mother with her own will to live. Right? So was it really a suicide attempt? Had there been enough pills to do the job? And, if so, why hadn't they done the job?

Often in suicide cases the attempt was more a half-assed effort, really more a cry for help. When one wanted to commit suicide, there were more successful ways and means—and instantaneous too. Jumping off a bridge to a highway of cement below was usually a guaranteed way. Taking a handful of pills, not so much.

Using all the bits and pieces she knew so far, trying to fit them together, drove Raina crazy. She hopped to her feet and paced.

Finally her name was called. She turned to see a doctor standing in the doorway. "How is my mother?"

He frowned. "She's still in very serious condition. We've pumped out her stomach, and we've given her something to stabilize her. She's on oxygen at the moment because her breathing was compromised."

At every word Raina's heart sank. "So she really did try to kill herself?"

The doctor shrugged. "Unless somebody force-fed her the pills, I don't know what else to tell you."

She pressed a hand against her temple. "I guess you see a lot of family members who look at you in complete shock and say, 'There's no way they would have done that' …"

He nodded. "Unfortunately that's very true. People seem to have an inner life that nobody else knows about. Was your mom depressed?"

"Not recently. At least not that I know of. My sister was murdered during the night. I was at Mom's house to tell her, and that's when I found her."

"So maybe someone else told her?"

"Possibly."

"Were they close?"

"Yes," she whispered. "Very close."

"Then there's your most likely explanation," he said. "She probably wouldn't have done this under normal circumstances, but, given the intense emotional shock, that would likely push her over the edge."

With that he left, leaving Raina once again full of dark thoughts. If her mother had found out, how? Who could have possibly told her?

She walked to the front desk and asked the receptionist, "Do you have my mother's personal belongings? I can't find her cell phone."

The woman looked up at her in surprise and then walked to the paper bag on the back counter. She checked it out and returned. "Here they are."

Raina went through it. When she found her mother's phone, she pulled it out and smiled. "This is what I need. Thank you." Not giving the other woman a chance to argue, she returned to the waiting room and sat down. She checked her mother's call history. There were several phone calls. One was from Annemarie, made early this morning.

Frowning, she picked up her phone and called Reyes. When he answered, she said, "Something is odd about the call history on my mom's cell phone."

"What?"

"The last call to my mother was from your mother this morning."

She heard the catch in Reyes's voice as he sucked in his breath. "Interesting," he murmured. "She didn't say anything about that earlier."

"Can you find out if she called my mom and said anything to her? Did she break the news to her?" She could hear the edge building in her tone. "I really wouldn't appreciate it if she did that. My mother shouldn't hear such news over the phone, and she shouldn't have been left alone afterward."

"No," he said, "it wasn't Annemarie's place. Let me talk to her and see." He hung up.

She hated to place that burden on him, but Annemarie was not the easiest of people in the first place. What Raina didn't know was how long those pills had been in her mother's stomach. The police had arrived at the restaurant about eight o'clock with the news about Reana. It was noonish when Raina had arrived at her mother's house. If the doctor confirmed that the pills were in her stomach for four hours or less, then chances were her mother had ingested the pills after the phone call Annemarie had made to her mom. And that had been the last call on her phone today.

Raina could feel anger, irrationally maybe, but still a burning anger that somebody might have broken the news to her mother. It was for the police or the next of kin to do. But then the police should have contacted her mother first too. Instead they'd come to the restaurant, hoping to catch the killer. She understood their reasoning, but someone else should have gone to her mother's place.

At that, she straightened and looked out the window. She didn't know for sure that another cop hadn't been at her mom's place. Frowning, she pulled out the business card the officer had given her at the restaurant and made a call. When he answered, he sounded distracted. She identified herself and then asked, "Can you please tell me if somebody went to my mother's house to let her know about my sister's death?"

"I might be able to find out. Why?"

"I don't know if you've heard yet, but we did tell the other officers to contact you about it. My mother supposedly attempted suicide this morning, and I want to know how she knew about my sister's death or if her suicide attempt was completely unrelated to my sister's murder."

His voice lowered with compassion. "I'm so sorry."

"So am I," she said, "but I need to know whether the police did a notification. Mom's in the hospital, and I am too. She's had her stomach pumped, and she'll survive the overdose, but she's still in a delicate state."

"I'll check and get back to you." And he hung up.

That was probably the best she could hope for at this point.

Still it sucked. As soon as she was allowed to, she went into her mother's little cubicle and sat down on the chair beside her bed. Raina held her mother's hand, gently stroking her fingers back and forth. "Mom, it's okay. No matter what's happened, it'll be okay."

She kept talking to her for a long moment and then realized there was absolutely no response, so she laid her mother's hand gently across her belly and just waited at her bedside. She continued to go through her mother's cell phone, seeing if anything else was going on that maybe Raina didn't know about. She didn't want to think of it as encroaching on her mother's privacy, but, if her mother had a relationship that Raina didn't know about or if something else was happening that upset her to this extent, then Raina needed to know.

She hated feeling like she was snooping, but she went back several days, then read forward. Instead of Reana discussing her sexuality, Reana discussed Reyes's return. And how she was worried and upset about it.

That blew Raina away because there was absolutely no need for this response. Reyes had no intention of even seeing her. Reana had kept silent about the real reason for their breakup. Given that, it made sense she'd be worried about what Reyes might say to set everyone straight.

Her mom's texts to Reana had reassured her that Reyes

would likely not even talk to her. It had been two years, so why would he? Or, at least if he did, it would be as if everything had changed and how they were friends now. Reana made it clear that she didn't want that. She wanted him *not* to talk to her, but she also didn't want him to talk to anybody in her circle.

Raina continued to read through the text messages between mother and daughter but found nothing earth-shattering. She went to the other text messages and found one from a boyfriend from a few years ago. He'd contacted her a month ago, asking about going out. She'd suggested coffee, and a date was set, which was in two days.

Raina frowned as she thought about that. "Why would she commit suicide if going on a date in a couple days?"

Or had she been so upset and distraught over her daughter's death that she didn't even think about the upcoming date? That sounded more likely.

After spending another twenty minutes on her mother's cell phone, Raina realized nothing here gave her any answers. She pocketed the phone and pulled out hers. As she did, it rang, and Reyes's number was displayed.

"Hey, what did you find?"

"Not much," he said. "My mom is pretty distraught."

"Yeah, I imagine," Raina said. "I called the officer to see if anybody there had gone to my mother's house, letting her know. He said he didn't think so, but he'd get back to me."

"Yeah," Reyes said. "Mom is not talking."

REYES REALLY HATED the fact that his mom wouldn't give him a straight answer. It made him very suspicious. After he hung up from Raina, he turned to look at his mom.

His dad held her close, shooting Reyes a hard look. "Surely we don't need to ask her any questions right now?" his father said.

"Yes, we do." Reyes stood his ground. "Mom, I need to know if you told Melissa about Reana's death."

He watched his mother's back stiffen. She spun on him in outrage.

But he refused to back down. This was way too important.

And, as she realized that, she started to cry again.

"Stop the waterworks," Reyes said sharply. "I love you dearly, but this is not the time for more dramatics. Melissa tried to commit suicide this morning. And we need to know who the hell had contact with her before that. We have a record of your phone call. Did you or did you not tell Melissa about Reana's death?"

His father turned to look down at Annemarie. "Please tell me that you're not the one who broke the news to her. That wasn't your job."

Annemarie looked up at him, her eyes huge, and she whispered, "I know, but I couldn't *not*. I figured she needed to know."

"No, you didn't think that at all," Reyes said. "As usual, you've stuck your nose where it didn't belong. And Melissa is now in the hospital in critical care from emptying every pill bottle she had in the house, trying to stop her pain. She shouldn't have been alone this morning—not to deal with that on her own."

At that, Annemarie burst into more tears and threw herself against her husband's chest. The two men glared at each other, but Reyes continued, "Dad, this is too damn important. We have a murdered young woman. We have another woman so distraught that she may have tried to commit suicide. And we have the third and final remaining family member who we need to know is not in any danger."

At that Reyes's father understood. "Yes, you're right," he said quietly. "I'm sorry. I was forgetting about Raina. She must be absolutely devastated."

"Not only did she find her mother almost dead," Reyes said, "but she took the blow of finding out about her sister this morning. She also had to identify Reana at the morgue. And then she went through her mom's cell phone to find out Mother had called Melissa. Mom, did you have any contact with Reana last night?"

His mom stiffened and turned to glare at him again. This time though she wiped her eyes free of moisture. "Are you accusing me of having anything to do with Reana's death?" she asked.

This time he was gratified to hear she was at least being reasonable and understood how severe this was. "I'm not accusing you of anything," he said. "But, so far, you've not given me any answers."

"I don't have to justify myself to you," she snapped.

"No, you don't," Ice said, stepping into the office. "But, if you don't, you are permanently damaging a relationship I don't think you really want to lose."

Annemarie stiffened. Even Reyes was surprised at Ice speaking up. But then he shouldn't be. Ice understood people. She understood relationships like very few people he knew.

Annemarie stared at Ice with a frown on her face. "What does my son accusing me of murder have to do with a relationship I want to keep?" she asked stiffly. "And this has nothing to do with you."

"That's not true," Ice said. "Because I was here during the last meeting between Reyes and Reana. Somewhere between that meeting and first thing this morning, when her body was found, that young woman was murdered. That was followed immediately by her own mother trying to commit suicide. So, before the police look to the mother for means and a reasonable motive for killing her own daughter, we have to find out exactly who the players are in this game. Your son is only trying to get to the bottom of this. So stop stonewalling and give him the answers he needs, or let's all go to the police station, where you can give them the answers they need," she said in a cool voice.

There was silence in the store, so everyone could hear Annemarie's answer. She stared at Ice in horror and then turned to look at her son.

He crossed his arms over his chest and waited.

"Yes, I spoke to Melissa. Yes, I told her about Reana's death. Sally from the restaurant called me this morning after hearing the news. No, I'm not happy with myself. I don't like that I did that. I should have waited for the police or for a family member to give that notice. But Melissa and I have been friends for a long time. We were almost sisters by marriage, if Reana and Reyes had married. I did feel I was a close-enough familial connection that I should tell her, but I can see now how that was a mistake. I can also see it shouldn't have been done over a phone call, nor should she have been alone at that time. Once I hung up, honestly I got so busy that I never thought about Melissa again. And that makes me feel very small."

She took a deep, shaky breath and added, "The last time I saw Reana was here in the office. I stood up to her yesterday for her behavior toward you, Reyes. And I spoke to her later that afternoon. She is my bookkeeper and accountant. And that'll cause its own set of problems. But I did not have any contact with her last night, overnight or this morning." She turned to glare at Ice. "Good enough?"

Ice nodded her head in a regal motion and said, "For the moment, yes." She studied Annemarie, stepped closer to her. "I only do business with owners and individuals"—she tilted her head at Reyes—"who are honest and forthright. If you, Annemarie, can't be direct without being forced to divulge information necessary to keep your son from being charged with murder, then I doubt I can trust you with any business transaction. I'll happily find another garden center to work with. Especially when you are putting Reyes in danger here as well."

Annemarie's shocked silence was heavy in the room.

"So get your ducks in a row—or not." Ice ignored Annemarie and her potential dramatic response and turned to Reyes. "How are we in tracking Reana's movements after being here yesterday?"

Reyes nodded. "Vince located her phone in her apartment last night. And she made several phone calls from that phone to her sister earlier in the evening. Speaking of which," he said, thinking hard, "Raina did say she read several text messages between her sister and her mother on her mother's phone. We need to know when those were made, so we can fit them in the overall time line." He pulled out his phone and dialed Raina again. "When were the text messages completed between your sister and your mother?"

"Just a sec," she said. "I'm looking. ... They were finished by six o'clock yesterday evening."

"And when did your mother last call you about your sister?"

"About seven or seven-thirty last night."

"And would she have really worried in that hour or so in between calls that Reana hadn't contacted her?"

"Their text messages ended a bit roughly, so, yes. Mother probably called to apologize, to make sure everything was okay," Raina said. "Nothing new from Reana since then is on her phone."

"So you're the last one to speak directly to Reana on the phone."

"Depends on what her phone says," Raina said. "I'm the last one to speak to her that I know about."

"Good point. The police have her phone. Vince handed it over, but I believe he said the last call was to you."

"So then they should be able to answer that question. Do you want to call them, or should I?"

"I'll call to confirm," Reyes added. "We need an update on the investigation also."

"And get a confirmation on time of death, please," Raina asked, her voice deepening with sorrow. "Even though I saw the bullet hole, do we know for sure that's how she died?"

"I'll ask," he said. He hung up, walked a few feet away and called the detective. As soon as he answered, Reyes identified himself and asked for an update. "We also need the time of death."

"I don't have much for you yet. The last person she spoke with on the phone was her sister. That confirmed Raina's story."

"Right. And there should have been a bunch of text messages before that with her mother, correct?"

"Yes, that's correct."

In the background Reyes could hear keyboard *click*s as the detective brought up reports. His change in attitude to

Reyes once again made him think Ice had said something to the detective.

"They've put her death at around midnight. She was beaten and then shot."

"Any line on finding her girlfriend?" Reyes asked.

"No," the detective said. "Maybe I should be asking you that question."

"I haven't had a chance to even start on that," Reyes said. "We went to drop off Raina, so she could talk with her mom about her sister's death, and found her mother had tried to commit suicide. Or so it looks like. Right now Raina is at the hospital."

"Right. I spoke with my partner. She called him. That's a sad situation."

"I know. In the meantime there was something odd at her house. In the main bedroom upstairs, the glass balcony doors were open. Melissa was terrified of intruders. She would never have slept with the doors open."

"But she didn't sleep, did she? It was morning. She had the doors open, and chances are she took the drugs this morning, after finding out about her daughter."

"Sure, but she was in the bedroom, and those balcony doors were always locked."

"So what are you saying? Somebody forced those drugs down her throat?"

"I don't know what I'm saying," Reyes said in frustration. "It's yet another anomaly."

"They happen," the detective said. "At this point, we're more concerned about finding her daughter's killer than worried about what might have happened with the mother. If we get any proof that she didn't commit suicide, then we'll look into that. But, at the moment, it looks like she was lost in grief and tried to take her own life. That's sad, but it happens."

As he hung up and put away the phone, Reyes agreed. He turned and explained the little he had learned to everyone in the office. Then he addressed Ice. "I don't know what you want to do about going home," he said, "but I want to stay. So I'll rent a vehicle for a couple days and see what I can find. I really need to find Reana's girlfriend."

"You have no name, no face, nothing?"

"No," he said. "Nothing. So I want to talk to Reana's other friends. Somebody will know something."

Ice pulled a set of keys from her pocket. "This is for you to use. Once we get the plants sorted out"—Ice sent a determined glare Annemarie's way—"I'll take my father's offer to fly them all back to Texas. We're not leaving for at least two days. So, if you can solve this in the meantime, perfect. If not, we'll put you on a commercial flight to get you home that way. In the meantime, this key is for a Jeep Wrangler. It's one of my dad's spare vehicles that he keeps around for us, and it's yours while you're here."

He stared at the keys, then at her, and a big grin cracked his face. "Your dad's the best."

She smiled. "I know. Just keep remembering that too. Family is important, whether it's immediate or extended. We do the best we can for them." These final words were addressed to Reyes's mother in particular.

Annemarie had enough sense to feel shame and guilt, if her facial expressions ran true.

# Chapter 9

RAINA DIDN'T KNOW where the afternoon went. She half dozed, but she kept jerking awake, checking on her mother often.

Finally at about four o'clock, her mother surfaced and smiled up at her. Raina jumped to her feet and leaned over her. "Hey, how are you feeling?"

"A little worse for wear," her mother whispered. "But I'm alive."

"The question is, is that a good thing or not?" Raina asked.

Her mother frowned, not understanding the question.

"Mom, did you try to commit suicide?"

Her mom stared at her. Then, all of a sudden, remembering about Reana, tears filled her mom's eyes. Melissa cried, first gently, then deep racking sobs came, turning her body into a frail old woman completely broken down by grief. "Reana," she whispered when she could. "Dear God. Please tell me it's not true."

Raina gripped her mother's hands and whispered, "I'm so sorry. But it is true."

Her mother curled up into a ball and motioned for Raina to leave. "Just go away," she whispered. "I can't deal with this. Please go away." She pulled the covers up over her face, hiding most of it.

Raina sat back down for a moment, not sure what to do other than notify a nurse. She exited the room to the main emergency area and told the first medical person she saw that her mother was awake.

The nurse went to check on her, but her mother had fallen back into a heavy sleep again.

Raina explained what Melissa had said, trying to stop the hurt from being too obvious.

The nurse gave her a gentle smile. "She's caught up in her own grief right now. She's not trying to hurt you. But she is not ready to live with her new reality."

Raina understood. It was pretty rough for her too. But her needs weren't important apparently. She shoved her hands in her pockets and said, "I don't know what to do now."

"Go home," the nurse said firmly. "You've spoken to her. You know we'll care for her and help her pull through. Just give her time and space."

Taking the nurse at her word, and feeling bruised inside and out, Raina went outside the front of the hospital and stood, staring up at the cloudy skies. It was hard to imagine this hurt ever going away. But she'd always understood there'd been something special between her mother and her sister. Raina knew in her heart of hearts that her mother wished it had been Raina who was dead, not Reana.

As soon as that thought came, Raina tried to stop herself from heading down that dark hole. It had been a great source of sadness and depression during her teenage years, and she'd finally gotten over it, realizing that was just the way of it. There was nothing she could do but accept it.

As she wondered what she was supposed to do now, a vehicle drove up. Reyes honked the horn at her, and she opened the passenger side door. "How did you know I was ready to leave?"

"I didn't," he said, "but I was coming to drag you away anyway. Pretty rough in there, huh?"

"Well, at least Mom woke up," she said shortly.

She expected him to drive away, but he didn't. He stayed and stared at her a long moment. Then he grabbed her fingers and squeezed them gently. "And?"

She tried hard not to break down, but, as soon as she explained what her mother had said, she could feel the tears cascading.

He turned the vehicle into a parking space and tugged her close. "You've been through a hell of a lot today and so has your mom. Just accept that, right now, she's not herself, and it's a tough time for everybody. You're doing what you can do."

"But how do you move forward, knowing your mother prefers your sibling, even after she's gone?"

"Easy," he said. "You suffer through it until it becomes something you can live with. I'm in the same boat. Mom and Ron are two separate people, and yet, they are two peas in a pod. They've always had a bond I never could access. I'm close to my father but not like those two are close. It's a very strange feeling growing up because you're always on the outside. You're the one who doesn't quite fit in."

She nodded. "Exactly. Maybe, if my father were still alive, I would have had what you have with yours, but it never seemed to be that way when he was with us."

"I don't really have much of a bond with my father. I love him dearly, but he's very over the moon with my mom, even now," he added with a grin. "I guess that's how it's supposed to be in a marriage that works," he said quietly.

"When I left two years ago, I hadn't realized what a burden my family was, how much of my life I was trying to live up to their expectations. I knew they loved me, in their own ways." He gave her a crooked grin. "But those teenage years are hell on feeling like you belong or are accepted."

She nodded. "I was just thinking that."

He released her so she could scoot back into her seat again. "Let's get some food."

"Did you learn anything from the police?" she asked as she buckled up and wiped away her tears.

Reyes put the transmission into drive and pulled out of the parking lot. "Not much. We'll talk about it over a meal. Then I thought you and I could go together to your mom's house and then to your sister's place, since I haven't managed to get to either place yet. I don't know how many answers there are anymore, but I really would like to find Reana's girlfriend, see if she's got anything to do with this."

"Fine. Food first."

He soon pulled into a popular Italian place. She smiled and said, "Yum, carbs would be perfect right now. Thank you."

The place was not very busy, as it was still early. They ordered right away, and the food came within a few minutes. She looked down at the large plate of spaghetti and said, "I almost feel guilty for eating. My sister is in the morgue, and here I am, trying to fuel up."

"That's how it always is. Those left behind have to deal with survivor's guilt. You can't change it that you are not the one lying in the morgue. You can't take your sister's place, and I, for one, am delighted you can't. Because I'd be afraid that you would try. And that's not the way to go. Your sister was a bright flame, but, like a lot of bright flames, they burn out very quickly. You have your whole life ahead of you. I would dearly love to see you enjoy some of it."

Part of her agreed, but another part still felt pretty emotionally rocked. She started to eat and was surprised to see her appetite returning. When she polished off her spaghetti in one steady session, she stared at her empty plate and then looked at him. "Wow. Okay."

He smiled. "Don't feel guilty about that now. You obviously needed the food."

She nodded and moved her plate off to the side. "I did. I'm feeling empty in many ways. I don't know when the police will release my sister's body, but I have funeral arrangements to take care of."

"Do you know what your mother wants to do about that?"

Raina shook her head. "No, and I'm not sure how long before my mom is capable of making those decisions."

Reyes nodded. "You'll figure it out," he said. "You don't have to make that decision today. You have several days, if not a full week."

"I doubt that," she said. "Definitely a couple days though." She picked up the glass of wine, wondering if it would help relieve her pain, then decided, after the day she'd had, it couldn't hurt. She took a sip and smiled. "I like this."

"It's a favorite of mine," he said with a smile. "I like my wines a little on the dry side. I was hoping you were okay with it."

"I didn't even realize you had ordered it," she said. "Most people would have chosen red with pasta."

He chuckled. "But red puts me to sleep, and right now that's the last thing I need. We'll go do some sleuthing. Then I'll take you home, so you can hopefully get a good night's sleep. Today was probably the worst day of your life, and tomorrow everything will be a little bit easier."

"I hope so," she said. "But I'm not so sure. There's still a whole lot to deal with."

He nodded. "If you're ready to go, I suggest we start with your sister's condo."

As they got up, he tossed money on the table to pay for the bill and a tip, and, with a hand on the small of her back, he nudged her toward the front door.

She glanced at her watch and exclaimed, "Feels like it's eleven at night, but it's only six."

"Exactly," he said. "Today has been a day of days, so it'll seem like it never ends. But, before it does, let's see if we can find something."

Once again he was driving, and this time he went straight to her sister's place. Raina stood outside the brownstone and wondered if her sister had left a will. Raina hated to even contemplate the financial aspect, but it had to be taken care of. And again she wondered how much help her mother would be. Hopefully the townhome went to her mother because she needed it. She still worked part-time because she didn't have quite enough money on her own.

Raina unlocked her sister's door, using the spare key she'd had since her sister bought the place, and went in. There was an eerie silence, a silence that said nobody was coming home ever again.

Slowly she walked down the hall into the kitchen. "I wonder how far Vince went in here?"

"He said her phone was sitting here on the counter." Reyes pointed to the empty counter.

She looked around in surprise. "This place is spotless. Reana was a bit of a perfectionist, but it was never quite this clean. I can't help but feel like it's been professionally cleaned." She sniffed the air. "I smell lemon cleanser."

He looked at her sharply. "Seriously?"

She nodded. "It's one my mom always used," she said. "It's like a Pine-Sol cleaner."

He walked to the sink area and opened cupboards and drawers. "Well, how about that?"

She turned to look. "What?"

"The cupboards are completely empty."

She frowned and went to the fridge, opened it and stared at the empty shelves that were perfectly cleaned too. She gasped. "The fridge is empty too. Did somebody move her out?"

"Maybe the better question is, did she actually live here?" he asked. "Or did she use it as a rental maybe?"

From the kitchen they went into the dining room and living room. There was no furniture. No table, no chairs, no couch, no recliners.

Raina stared in bewilderment. "I don't get it. Where's all her stuff? Did Vince say anything about it?"

He shook his head and called Vince. "Hey, was Reana's apartment empty?"

"Not completely but close. I figured she was moving."

After Reyes hung up, he told Raina, but she stared at him blankly.

"How long since you were here?"

She turned toward him. "I'm not sure," she said. "We haven't exactly been best friends."

"What about your mother?"

"I don't know. I guess we have to ask her. More questions to ask my mother," she said faintly. "If and when she's ready to answer them." She walked through to the bedroom and bathroom. "It's so damn clean. Either somebody has just emptied this place out, or Reana moved out earlier and didn't tell us."

"Both could be an option." He walked back to the front door and looked at the neighbors on either side. He turned toward her and said, "It's early enough that people should be home from work and yet not late enough to be in bed. I'll knock on the neighbors' doors and see what they have to say."

She joined him. At the first house there was no answer. At the second house, still in the same direction, a young woman answered. When Raina and Reyes explained who they were and asked when the neighbor had last seen Reana coming in or out of her place, the woman shrugged and said, "I haven't seen anybody in that place for a little while."

"Really? It's my sister's condo," Raina said. "As far as I knew, she was living here full-time."

The woman looked at her. "A woman has been living there for a couple years. Two of them. One I haven't seen for a week or so, and the other one just moved out," she said with a shrug. "I figured they'd had a blowup or something." She paused, took a better look at Raina. "One of the women looked like you. You did say you're twins, didn't you?"

Raina nodded. "Yes. Did the other woman have long curly hair?"

"Not so much curly but big waves, yes. Beautiful woman. Tall and slim," the woman said enviously. "I wish I had her figure."

"How long did she live here?" Reyes asked.

The woman shrugged. "I don't know. As far back as I can remember though. She took a load out today, probably the end of it, but I don't know." She moved a step back in and started to close the door.

Raina asked quickly, "You don't have any pictures of her, do you?"

The woman frowned. "Why? It's your sister and her friend. Don't you have pictures?"

Raina looked over at Reyes, and he shrugged. "It's not for public knowledge at the moment, but her sister was murdered. And we're trying to find out who else was living here."

The woman's gasp was loud and harsh. "Murdered?"

They nodded. "Yes."

She glanced over at the brownstone in horror. "You don't think she was killed in there, do you?"

"No, I don't think so," Raina said immediately. "Do you know who the other woman was?"

"I don't know what her name was. But we did get some mail for that address. Just a second."

She closed the door behind her, leaving them standing on the front step.

She returned a few minutes later and handed over a piece of mail. "The letter is addressed to Jenny Bengals."

Raina looked at the delivery address, and it was her sister's, but, more than that, it had her own mother's address in the return address spot. So her sister had moved back in with her mom? Was that possible? Maybe if Reana was going through a breakup, she'd move out temporarily. Raina asked, "Do you mind if we take this?"

"Be my guest," the woman said. "I guess I'd have given it to the police anyway."

"We will," Reyes said.

The woman nodded and closed the door without saying anything else.

They walked back down the stairs toward his Jeep, and Raina said, "I don't know that name. How is it my sister had a whole life we knew nothing about?"

"I'm pretty sure it's because she had a different lifestyle that she thought other people wouldn't approve of."

"Maybe," Raina said. "It's hard to know. But, now that we have a name, I suggest we try to find Jenny."

Back in the vehicle, Reyes leaned over into the back seat and pulled his laptop forward. "Let's see if we can track her down." He opened the laptop and started a search.

She stared at the envelope. "I want to open it."

"Then do it." He looked over at the letter. "Your mother is in no shape to deal with this. And your sister's death makes you her guardian of sorts. Why not open it?"

She ripped it open and pulled out a single handwritten sheet. She gasped.

"What's the matter?"

"It's from my sister," she said. "Mailed to this Jenny Bengals."

"What does it say?"

Raina read it through, the tears gathering in her eyes as she saw the painful words her sister felt compelled to put down on paper. "She wants Jenny back. She said Jenny is the only person she's ever loved, and she's sorry she's such a coward. But she wants her back and agrees to going public with their relationship."

"That's interesting. At least that adds credence to the fact Reana had a female lover."

"But why didn't she tell us?" Raina raised her gaze to look at Reyes. "She could have told me."

"But she didn't tell you much, did she? She kept you out of that part of her life, correct?"

Raina nodded. With a sad smile she said, "Yes. We were hardly your typical sisters."

"Your sister was also extremely confident as a woman. She had a lot of personal power. I think she liked the way other people saw her. If people knew she was gay, it would have changed that. Or she assumed it would."

"It wouldn't have mattered to me," Raina said painfully. She got to the end of the letter, realizing her sister's heart was breaking. "She must have known Jenny was gone. What did she think would happen to this letter?"

"More to the point, when did this letter come? Because it might have been delivered to the wrong house before Jenny left."

"And that would be very heartbreaking for my sister to be waiting on a response. At the end of the letter, she says, 'Please call me. Please. Don't just walk away and leave me like this.'" Even the words made Raina choke. So much pain in such a short time. "Surely something could have been done."

"For all you know, Jenny is the one who killed her," Reyes said.

She shook her head. "If it's the same woman she was sleeping with when you found them together, then it's at least a two-year-old relationship."

"You also have to realize that passion is often a killer in itself. We must find out who this Jenny person is." He clicked a few more buttons on his laptop keyboard.

She looked at the letter. This had been heartbreaking for her sister, who was living a lie, living a life so full of deception that she must have been very confused as to what she really desired and how to make the sacrifice so she could have everything she wanted.

"If this is the same woman," he said, "and it's got your sister's condo address on it, she works at a local PR company. She has done some modeling, and she's known for her copywriting experience."

She stared at him. "Seriously?"

He nodded. "Why? Does that ring a bell?"

"Maybe. Reana used to talk about this guy, Jamie." She looked down at the name Jenny. "He had a PR company. I wonder if it's the same person? She wouldn't have been using a guy's name for her sexual partner, would she? Unless to hide the relationship?"

"I have no clue. How did Reana have a relationship with a PR company?"

"That's easy. They were one of her clients."

"That makes sense. And somehow, somewhere along the line, she and Jenny hit it off. Actually ..." His voice trailed off as he continued to type on his laptop. "Jamie and Jenny appear to be brother and sister. He works at the same company."

"I suggest we talk to them because, if nothing else, we need to track down Jenny. She may or may not want to see this last letter," she said, "but we certainly need to get a few answers from her."

He looked at the address on his computer screen. "I highly doubt they're open right now."

"Maybe. But is there a phone number?"

He snatched his phone and dialed the office number. He was surprised when somebody answered. "Hey, this is Reyes, a friend of Reana's. Is there any chance Jenny is working late today?"

"We're all working late today," said a peevish woman at the end of the phone. "We've got a marketing project that's not going well. Can I get her to call you back?"

"Yeah. Tell her it's very important, please. She should know the name—Reyes." He hung up the phone and placed it on top of the laptop and waited.

The two stared at each other.

Then the phone rang.

HE PICKED UP the phone and said, "Hello, Jenny. I'm a friend of Reana's family." He took a deep breath. "In fact, I'm Reyes, her ex-fiancé. We might have met once, in less-than-ideal circumstances."

Silence followed on the other end. "How did you find me?" she asked abruptly.

"We were just at Reana's condo. We found out you've moved recently."

"She said she'd never tell anybody," Jenny said, her voice faintly surprised. "What made her change her mind?"

"Can we meet you? Some of this news is a little difficult. And we have a few questions we need to ask."

"Why?" she asked with suspicion. "It's been two years since I saw you, and I can't say it was a great visit then."

"Reana's sister is here with me. Please, can we meet somewhere?"

Jenny hesitated and then said, "There's a Starbucks at the corner of the office building. I'll meet you there in ten." She hung up.

He looked up the Starbucks and turned on the engine. "Let's go. If nothing else, we're about to meet the most important person in your sister's life."

Raina shot him a hard look. "I'm still stumped. Until your arrival yesterday, I had no clue Jenny even existed."

"Life is like that sometimes," he said. "Now we just have to go with the flow and try to fill in all the blanks."

It took ten minutes to drive to the Starbucks. He pulled into the back parking lot, and they walked inside. He stood in the doorway to see if Jenny was already here. But he saw no sign of her. He ordered two coffees, and they took a table in the corner. As they waited, he kept his gaze searching the small coffee shop.

And suddenly a gasp came from behind Reyes. Raina looked up to see a woman staring at her. Raina quickly stood. "I'm Raina. Not Reana."

The look of relief and pain that crossed Jenny's face made Reyes realize just how important their relationship had been to her. "Please, would you sit down?" He motioned at an empty chair beside them.

She sagged into the chair as if her legs wouldn't hold her up any longer.

Reyes gave her a moment and then said, "May I buy you a coffee?"

"No, no. I'm fine, thank you." She asked Raina, "Why are you here?"

"When was the last time you spoke with Reana?"

Jenny glanced at her phone. "It's been at least a week. We had a final fight. She'd moved her personal belongings out right afterward to give me time to move out without her underfoot. The furniture was mostly mine, and she wanted me to take.everything away, so it wouldn't hurt her so much to see it. She said she'd start again with new furniture later. Once I started moving out, we severed all ties."

"Were you expecting to hear from her before you moved?"

Jenny's lips curled. "Let's say, I was hoping to. I was

hoping your sister would choose us over her current life. But she didn't."

Raina pulled the letter from her purse and handed it to her. "We were just over at her condo, and the neighbor had this letter that was misdelivered. Since you'd moved out, she didn't know what to do with it. It's a letter from my sister to you."

The woman stared at her, looked at the envelope, slowly pulled out the letter and started to read. Tears collected in the corner of her eyes, and she looked up. "Where is Reana? Why isn't she delivering this in person?"

Raina exchanged glances with Reyes.

Reyes leaned forward and softly said, "I'm sorry. Reana is dead."

Jenny shook her head. "No, no, no. That can't be." Her gaze frantically went from one to the other. "When? Why? How? I don't understand," she cried out. "Please, please, please tell me that's not so."

Raina took a deep breath. "We found out first thing this morning. And we don't have any answers. She was murdered."

Jenny stared at her, then seemed to lose all her stuffing. She sobbed, holding the letter tight against her heart.

Raina rubbed Jenny's shoulders, trying to make her feel better. When Jenny wound down slightly, Raina whispered, "I'm so sorry. I really am."

"And the police don't know who?"

Raina shook her head. "They're trying to figure it out, but we don't have any leads at the moment. They believe it was Reyes. When he told them how he'd broken off with her two years ago, you came up."

Jenny nodded. "That was always the big difficulty between us. Reana didn't want anybody to know. She didn't want anybody to know about me," Jenny said painfully. "Finally I couldn't take only living with part of her and gave her an ultimatum. And we decided to part ways." She held up the letter. "If you hadn't brought this, I would never have known she had changed her mind."

"Well, the good news is, she loved you," Raina said. "Unfortunately that doesn't bring us any closer to knowing who hated her enough to kill her."

Reyes studied the stunning woman in front of him. Grief had taken a toll, and even now he was amazed Jenny could function. But he found no deceit in her gaze, and her fingers trembled with shock as she came to grips with the fact that not only had Reana wanted to get back with Jenny and to tell the world the truth but also that Reana was now gone forever. Reyes asked her, "Any idea who might have wanted her dead?"

"No," Jenny whispered. "I really don't know." She stole a look at Reyes. "She was pretty upset after you found us."

"I was pretty upset myself," Reyes said in a laconic voice. "It's not only that she was cheating on me but that she was cheating with another woman."

"I understand that too," Jenny confessed. "When I first met her, she didn't tell me that she was engaged. But even then I knew our attraction was too strong to ignore. The thing is, it wasn't just a physical thing." She waved her hand. "I really loved her." Her expression became defiant, and she asked, "Did you?"

"No," Reyes said calmly. "I realized, after we broke up, that I really didn't. We were like oil and water. And I spent my childhood with that kind of relationship with my mother, which is probably what the attraction had been in the first place with Reana. She reminded me very much of my mother. A mother I'm still trying to have a close relationship with. And maybe that is part of the problem. I thought maybe, if I couldn't have it with my mother, I could have it with my wife. Because my mother and father are happy."

Jenny looked at him for a long moment. "That makes sense. She did say something about the fact that she and Annemarie were similar."

"*Very* similar," Raina said quietly. "They're both very volatile, very passionate, very dramatic women. For both Harold, his father, and for Reyes, it's been a bit of a trial being with them."

"She wasn't like that with me," Jenny said. "Reana was always very calm, considerate. There was almost a sense of peace around her."

"I'm glad to hear that," Reyes said, "That probably means she was happy. I'm glad she found a sort of peace with you."

"But that would mean your father isn't good for your mother, if we follow that line of thought through," Raina said. "Or maybe it was just true for Reana and you."

"My parents have had plenty of difficulties," Reyes said. "It's one of the reasons why I found it hard to get along with my mother all this time. She was always really rough on my father. I found that difficult growing up."

"Your brother, Ron, is very much like Reana and Annemarie too," Raina said.

He nodded. "Did you guys have friends outside of your relationship?"

"Not really," Jenny said. "We kept to ourselves, didn't have friends in common. We didn't go out with other friends because nobody knew about us. My brother knew, of course, and I had an ex-girlfriend who knew. And then there were potentially other boyfriends in Reana's life who she didn't tell me about," she admitted. "I wanted her to be completely honest with me, but I don't think she was."

"I knew of at least a Jack and a Tom and a Larry," Raina said. "But again, I don't know how much of a relationship she had with them. I just know she talked about going out with them."

Reyes watched pain whisper across Jenny's face. "You recognize those names?"

She nodded. "We did have one fight in particular. And she said she would go out and have more relationships, so she could forget me." Jenny stared out the window. "Whereas I stayed inside my little turtle shell and tried to heal, she went out and dated pretty extensively for a little while, almost as if proving she were 'normal.'"

"Men were always extremely starstruck with her," Raina said. "Any chance one of those men didn't want her to break it off? Maybe threatened her?"

"Not that I knew of," Jenny said. "Although I'm not sure we were exclusive then, so it wasn't my business."

"Was she ever exclusive?" Reyes asked curiously. "Because I never got the feeling she was with me."

"I'd like to think so." Jenny's voice and smile were gentle. "I truly believe we had something special, a love that would last. She just had to deal with the fact that some of the world would have trouble with our relationship."

"And that, of course, is where the problem was," Raina said. "We're looking for anybody who might have had a motive for killing her."

Jenny sagged in front of them. "I can't imagine why anybody would want to. She was so full of life."

"That often brings out the best and the worst in people," Reyes said. "If it was a man who didn't want to shut down a relationship, a fight—especially in a volatile relationship, like Reana often preferred—could have turned deadly quickly."

"How was she killed?"

"Beaten and shot," Raina said quietly. "I didn't get any details about how long before the bullet the bruises were there."

Jenny's lower lip trembled. "I don't even know anyone with guns."

"Unfortunately a lot of people do." Reyes's voice was a little harsher. "How many other people knew her?"

Jenny looked surprised briefly. "You mean, how many people in my world knew about her?"

He nodded.

"Not many. My brother, an ex as I said before, and I have a couple girlfriends I used to go to and cry on their shoulders when Reana and I had difficulties. They're another gay couple, Susan and Brenda. They knew about her."

"Is there any chance they would have had anything to do with her death?" Raina asked, leaning forward.

Jenny shook her head vehemently. "Oh, no. They're not that type of people at all. They're very gentle, and they didn't know her personally. They just knew of her. And, yes, they were definitely angry at her at times. Angry at the way she treated me," Jenny said defiantly. "And they kept telling me how I shouldn't go back to her. Once they understood I really loved her and would do anything to make it work, then they were there for me."

"Who helped you move out?" Reyes asked.

"My brother. He also helped me buy my new home. It's another townhome but closer to work, closer to him."

"Do you know anything about Reana's financial situation?" Raina asked. "About her will?"

Jenny stared at her in surprise. "No, I don't. I presume everything would go to you and your mother."

"I don't know," Raina said. "It's possible. But it could also be that you're listed too."

"Great," Jenny said. "That'll have the police crawling all over me."

"You'll have to talk to the police anyway," Reyes said. "I told them about finding the two of you in bed, that that was the reason for my breaking it off with Reana two years ago. They were determined to pin her murder on me and didn't believe she had a girlfriend."

Jenny nodded. "Of course I'll talk to them," she said wearily. "Hopefully they'll find out who did this and fast." She started to stand.

"Will you please talk to them soon?" Raina asked impulsively. "We could go to the station with you."

Jenny stopped in the act of straightening up. She stared at them both. "This is really important, isn't it?"

"Very," Reyes said in a rough tone. "The police are seriously looking at me. And, while they're looking at me, they're not looking for who really killed her."

Jenny thought for a moment, then nodded. She glanced around the coffee shop. "Can we do it now then, before I lose my nerve?"

Raina jumped to her feet. "Absolutely. Why don't we all go in our vehicle, and then we'll drive you back to yours."

She hesitated and then shook her head. "I'll feel better if I have my own wheels."

"I understand that," Raina said. "I'll come with you, and we'll meet Reyes there." She glanced at Reyes. "Are you okay with that?"

Reyes hesitated. He wasn't exactly sure why, but something about the situation didn't feel right. Yet he could find no obvious problem. What they really had to do was get Jenny to the police station. But what if Jenny had killed Reana, and now he was leaving Raina alone with Jenny?

"That's fine," he said slowly. "I'll follow the two of you."

They rose and exited the coffee shop. He got into his Jeep, waiting for the two women to get into the small Audi Jenny drove. He noted the vehicle and realized she didn't appear to be suffering for money if she drove a car like that.

The trip was slow. Lots of traffic, as it was now just after eight in the evening, and rush hour was still heavy. With his cell phone mounted on the dash, he called Ice and brought her up to date.

"Well, that's great that you found Jenny," Ice said. "The guys have already started tracking the cameras around the brownstone from six o'clock forward to see what Reana's movements were last night. So far nothing concrete is showing up. Her phone didn't end up there on its own." Ice spoke to someone in the room with her. "We're on this. You get to the police station and have Jenny confirm your story. That'll go a long way to having the police back off of seeing you as their main suspect."

"That's what I'm hoping," he said. "But there's still likely to be a lot of resistance to letting me go as I seem to be their *only* suspect."

"They don't have any reason to hold you," she said.

"Did you get to the store? To sort through the plants?"

"Your mother apologized to me. Seemed sincere. She's supposed to tell you that she's sorry too." Ice chuckled. "I've been talking with my dad here, and we have a big list of plants we think will do well. I'll talk to your father tomorrow and see what he might have available."

"That would be good," Reyes said. "I keep hoping this headache will have a quick resolution, but I'm not so sure it will be."

"It doesn't matter how long it takes," she said firmly. "Life happens when we least expect it." On that note she ended the call.

Still smiling, he followed the women to the police station. They both parked in the back lot. He got out and waited for them to join him. Jenny looked even more unhappy at the idea of approaching the police station. He stepped up, slipped an arm through both women's arms and said, "I really appreciate you doing this, Jenny."

She sighed. "You don't need to worry that I'll run away. I have to do this for Reana's sake, if nothing else."

"I'm sorry she was never open about your presence in her life," Raina said. "It would have been nice to have known you years ago."

Jenny nodded. "That's what I told her. All those years we wasted were years we could have bonded as a family."

"How did your brother feel about your relationship?"

"He didn't particularly like it much," Jenny said. "Not because it was a lesbian relationship—because that's what I've always had, and he has accepted that—but I think it was more because of Reana herself."

"They didn't get along?" Raina asked in surprise. "Everybody gets along with Reana."

"The problem was, she flirted with him," Jenny said. "I knew it was just her way, but my brother didn't take it so well. He saw it more as a betrayal of her relationship with me. He also didn't understand how Reana could want to be with both men and women at the same time."

"That's because life is never as clear-cut as we'd like to think it is," Reyes said.

Inside the station, he walked up to the reception desk and asked to speak to Detective Burgess.

The harried receptionist looked at Reyes and sent a message announcing him. He walked back to the bench seating and sat down. It took a good ten to fifteen minutes, to the point he wondered if he would have to return to the front desk and ask again, before Detective Burgess walked out.

He raised an eyebrow. "What can I do for you?"

Reyes could feel Jenny stiffen beside him. Reyes stood and said, "I'd like you to meet Jenny Bengals. This is Reana's lover. And she has been since I found them in bed over two years ago."

The detective's gaze turned on Jenny. He studied her for a long moment. "Is that true?"

Jenny nodded. "Yes, it is. I've been moving out of her place this last week. It's been a week since I spoke to Reana."

He led them into a small room, where he asked the three of them a bunch more questions. It wasn't anything new as far as Reyes was concerned. But he wasn't sure from the look on Raina's face.

He turned and whispered, "Are you okay?"

The detective focused on her. "Is something else bothering you?"

Raina hesitated and then nodded. "Actually there is."

# Chapter 10

RAINA WASN'T EXACTLY sure how to explain it. She looked at Jenny. "Do you have any idea if Reana said something to my mother?"

Jenny frowned. "I don't think she did. Your mother was one of the concerns that held Reana back from going public. You and your mother."

"Me?" Raina asked in surprise. "I would have been totally okay with it."

Jenny studied her for a long moment and then gave a clipped nod. "I believe you, but Reana didn't. She said she had an image to uphold, and she wouldn't have taken your laughter and mockery well."

Raina stared at her. "I would never have mocked her for making a life choice like that. All I ever wanted was for her to be happy. And I wasn't exactly sure that she would ever be happy, being the person she was. She was always very critical and judgmental."

"And again I think that was just with you," Jenny said. "With me, she was a very different person. If you can imagine, we used to play an awful lot of computer games together. Also we liked watching movies and eating popcorn. We spent hours and hours together just talking, doing our nails, spending time together. It wasn't a competition between us. I think she always felt that she had to compete with you."

Raina sagged in her chair. "Are you serious? There was no competition. She was always the best, the oldest, the prettiest, the smartest ..."

Jenny laughed out loud. "And she would have said that she wasn't in any way those things, that something was wrong with her because she was gay, that she wasn't very smart, and that's why she was so loud. She was always trying to cover up, trying to distract people from seeing her insecurities. Whereas you were always quiet and confident. You stayed in the background because you were okay to be in the background. She wasn't. She was always trying to eclipse you because everyone loved and admired you. So she was louder, bigger, brighter as a defense mechanism."

Raina felt like she'd been struck across the face. She stared at Reyes and then back at Jenny. "Seriously?"

Jenny nodded. "Absolutely. She loved you to distraction, but she also said she hated you because of who you were. She wanted to be that same self-confident person, that person who was at peace on the inside, so she could walk through life and not get distracted and disturbed by everything going on around her. Everything upset Reana. Except when she was with me. During the time we spent together, it was like she could truly be herself, and she didn't have to put on all these different personas that other people expected from her."

"I can't believe that's what she was like with you," Raina said faintly. "How absolutely exhausting it must have been for her otherwise."

"And terrifying," Reyes said. "Is there anything worse than feeling like you'll be found out at any moment?"

Jenny looked at him and nodded. "Exactly. That's how

she felt all the time. She never could really relax and be who she was. She was completely stressed out, always believing something was wrong with her, and everybody would know. And that's what she couldn't face. She fully believed that she would lose her clients, that she would lose her friends. And everybody would mock her for her life choices."

"I'm so sorry to hear that," Raina said, "because it's not true. She was everything to me, and it's just so devastating to hear this. She never had to be like that. It was exhausting to be around her all the time. I always felt so inferior and so unloved. By my mother *and* Reana."

"And yet, that's how Reana felt as well. She felt like she wasn't 100 percent perfect, 100 percent beautiful, 100 percent on and vibrant and alive. If she wasn't, then something was wrong with her because everybody expected her to be that way. But she couldn't keep it up. So she would come to me. I would allow her to just drop it all and to become herself, not that I did anything special to make her feel that way. Sometimes she would just curl up in my arms and cry because it was so exhausting."

That brought tears to Raina's eyes. She clasped her hand over her mouth and wrapped her other arm around her chest. "That's so not how I would have wanted her to live," she whispered.

"I told her that. I told her that she needed to trust in who you were, that she needed to trust in the love of sisters and her mother. But she said her mother was the worst. Her mother felt something *was* wrong with people like us— therefore, with people like Reana. How your mother would never accept such a flaw in Reana."

"That's true," Raina said. "My mother has very strong feelings on that subject."

"Reana couldn't tell you in case your mother found out. She knew your mother wouldn't accept her as she was."

"But I would have understood," Raina cried out passionately. "Reana could have trusted me."

"But you had a different relationship with Reana than with your mother. There was still that jealousy because you were normal. Because you weren't lesbian." A sad bitterness in Jenny's tone broke Raina's heart.

"But that was a battle neither of us could win," Raina cried out. "She had you, and she felt so good with you, so calm and so at peace. It would have made such a difference in her life."

"Which is why that letter you gave me has helped in how I view her," Jenny said gently. "I'll grieve for what we could have had, but at least now I know she finally came around to loving me first and foremost."

"Letter?" the detective asked.

Raina realized he'd been listening to them all along. His gaze went from one to the other as they continued to discuss her sister and the broken relationships she had cultivated.

"We went to the neighbor's house, asking if they had seen my sister and when because the brownstone was completely cleaned out. The neighbor said Jenny had moved out, and a piece of mail had been misdelivered to her place. It was a letter for Jenny. And, yes, I opened it. It's through that letter we found out how to contact Jenny." She motioned to Jenny. "And, when we connected, I gave her the letter. It was my sister's apology, telling Jenny how much Reana really loved Jenny and that Reana was willing to go public to keep Jenny in her life."

"So I gather in all that, you didn't kill her?" the detective said bluntly to Jenny.

That startled a cry from her throat. "No," she said. "I loved her. She was everything to me."

"But she wouldn't become one with you, would she?" he said. "You moved out, broke up, so there had to be a lot of pain and anger."

Jenny shook her head. "Pain, yes. Anger, no. Just loss," she said quietly. "And grief, overwhelming grief. And now so much more grief. While Reana was alive, there was always hope she would come to her senses and return to me. But to know she did come to that point but is now gone, ... I'm not sure how or if I'll ever recover."

Reyes nodded. "I think we've all come to an understanding of who Reana was."

"That's all fine and dandy," the detective said, "but we're not getting any closer to knowing who killed her."

"She was badly bruised and beaten, you said. Did those occur at the same time? Or is it possible she was beaten up earlier and then shot later?"

"No, it was all at the same time," he said. "And the beating, although it showed up as lots of bruising—as you know, a lot of damage—it wasn't too extreme."

"Meaning, her attacker could have been a female?" Reyes asked.

The detective looked at him, assessing. "Yes, I suppose it could have been. It also could have been a guy who wasn't used to being violent. A boxer would have probably caused a lot more damage. This person, male or female, wasn't skilled in that way. It looked more like he took out his temper on her."

"And that would be so typical of the way she lived," Jenny said. "She seemed to do nothing but pick fights with everybody around her." She glanced over at Raina. "And that goes back to her not being happy with who she was. She was living a twisted life, wanting to be one way but forced to be another."

"But only forced in her own mind," Raina said wearily. "I'm trying to figure out what happened to my mother now too."

"What's wrong with your mother?" Jenny asked.

"She potentially tried to commit suicide this morning. And, yes, that was probably after hearing the news of Reana's death."

The detective nodded. "Nobody made that call here. I did check."

"No. We can put that down to my mother," Reyes said. "She broke the news to Melissa."

"That must have been devastating for her," Jenny said. "Did she not stay and help her for the first few hours?"

"Unfortunately my mother just made a phone call. And when I dropped off Raina, so she could break the news to her mother, Raina found her mom unconscious on her bed, having ingested several bottles of pills."

"That's terrible," Jenny murmured. "Not hard to understand though."

"It isn't, except for the fact that my mother was completely afraid of the glass balcony doors in her bedroom. They were always locked, and she kept a pole blocking the doors from being opened from the outside. But when we got there this morning, the doors were open and so was the window. That was incredibly unusual for her."

"So you think somebody was in there at that time? Or somebody was there beforehand?" Jenny asked in confusion. "I don't understand."

"Neither do I," Raina said with a heavy sigh. "And,

though I had a chance to speak to my mother, she wasn't very aware of her surroundings."

"No wonder." Jenny stared at Raina. "I'm so sorry. I've lost Reana, but you've lost both Reana and potentially your mother."

"My mother is expected to survive the overdose," Raina said quietly. "But I'm not sure mentally or emotionally she'll ever be the same again."

REYES CHECKED HIS watch, looked at the detective and asked, "Do you have what you need? I'd like to take Raina back to the hospital, so she can be with her mother."

The detective straightened and became more business-like. "Just a few more things here." He ripped through the next few questions and then said, "Okay, you two can go. We'll get Jenny to sign her statement, and then she can leave too."

Raina stood, addressing Jenny. "May I have your phone number to contact you, if needed? I still have my sister's estate to take care of."

Jenny nodded and shared her cell phone number. "And thank you," she said. "This letter means everything to me."

Raina smiled at her gently. "I'm glad I found it."

Reyes placed a hand on the small of her back and nudged her toward the doorway. There, he turned and smiled at Jenny. "Thank you very much for coming in." Then he stepped out.

As they walked back to the Jeep, Raina turned to look at him. "There's no reason not to believe what Jenny said, is there?"

"No," he said. "I feel fairly confident she's telling the

truth."

"I like her," Raina said with a smile. "It's so hard not knowing what happened."

"I know, but we have a whole new line of questions. There were men in Reana's life. Jenny didn't particularly like that, but that does give us other suspects."

"Only if we can figure out who they are."

"And now that we're not standing right beside Jenny," Reyes said, "I highly suggest we have a talk with her brother. He'll have a very different take on their relationship than Jenny has."

"Oh, that's a good idea," Raina said. "We should have asked her for his contact information."

"Don't have to. It's on the company website."

"I doubt we'll get in touch with him tonight. Maybe we can set up a meeting with him tomorrow."

At the Jeep, Reyes pulled out his laptop and checked for the number, then called. As he expected, there was no answer, so he left a message.

"He may or may not call us back tonight." He put the Jeep into gear and drove toward the hospital. "Now I'm the one who said we should go to the hospital, but, if you're not ready to, just speak up."

"What I need," she said, "is to find out why my mother did what she did. But I can't guarantee she'll be any closer to telling us the answer to that question."

"We also should go through your sister's condo again. I know Jenny lived there, but Vince did find your sister's cell phone. So, in some way, your sister—and possibly her murderer—had to have been there, potentially leaving clues behind."

"It's on the way to the hospital," Raina said impulsively.

"We can take a quick detour. That place is empty, so it's not like there'll be a whole lot to search through."

Reyes changed lanes and took the next left. A few blocks later, he pulled in front of the brownstone. "We've learned a lot since we were here last," he muttered. "Let's hope this time we get a bunch more answers."

As they walked up toward the front door, the neighbor was getting out of her car. She looked up and smiled. Raina walked over to her.

Reyes stuck close to her and said, "Thank you very much for that letter."

Raina said, "I passed it on to Jenny."

The neighbor's face lit up. "I'm glad to hear that. You were asking about any men ... There was one man. He appeared to be fairly close to the woman with the long brown hair, Jenny. I saw them hugging. He seemed to be quite concerned about her. At one point, I do recall seeing her crying on the front porch and him holding her, trying to soothe her. He left in some fancy little sports car," she said. "And, of course, I have absolutely no clue who he was. The woman went back inside when he left."

Reyes nodded and tucked that information in the back of his mind. He highly suspected it was Jamie. It didn't seem like Jenny had too many other male friends. Reyes snagged Raina's fingers with his own and said, "Thanks again."

The two walked over to the brownstone. They stood in the front hall, deciding where to search. He started at the front closet, checking the top shelf, running his hands down the walls, making sure no loose boards were on the floor. He went systematically through the rest of the house. The kitchen was completely empty, holding absolutely nothing of interest. The entire downstairs was empty.

When they got upstairs to the two bedrooms and the two bathrooms, it was the same story. In the master bedroom, they stopped and studied the empty room.

"When Jenny moved out, she moved out," Raina said with a smile. "As a tenant she must have been a godsend."

"I wonder if she was paying rent though," Reyes said. "But it's a good point."

"I highly doubt she murdered Reana over not wanting to pay rent," Raina said thoughtfully. "But I suppose murder has occurred for an awful lot less."

He glanced around at the floor. "If any foul play happened here, everything has been completely cleaned up. No sign of bloodstains. No smells that anything nasty occurred in this place."

"I know," she said. "When we first walked in, I held my breath, hoping I wouldn't smell anything bad. Now I'm actively trying to detect something and sense nothing." She turned to face Reyes. "With those last phone calls Reana made to me, do you think my sister was trying to tell me about Jenny? Or that she was in trouble when she called me over and over again?"

"That is likely a mystery we won't get an answer to. So let's fill in the details in a way you can live with. Maybe she was planning on telling you. That could have been her first step in convincing Jenny that Reana was serious. On another note, the police have Reana's vehicle. It would be nice to know if they think she was murdered there or if she was moved into her car and then left elsewhere."

"Will they tell us?"

He pulled out his phone. "Let's find out."

When he put his phone away ten minutes later, he shook his head. "They believe she was killed and placed in her vehicle and parked behind the coffee shop." He watched as her shoulders sagged.

"Ugh. I know I asked, but…"

"You can't blame them," he said, "but I might have a way around it."

He sent Ice a text, asking if she had any local connections who could find out if they had a primary crime scene and where it might be.

He received an answer almost immediately. He grinned. "See? There's a difference between law enforcement and the company I work for. Law enforcement basically says, *Get the hell out of their case*, and they won't tell us anything. Ice is like, *Let me check. I'll see if I have a source who can get that information for us. The police might want to hold it back from the media at this point*." He looked up, smiling to see Raina looking at him in surprise.

"Really? Ice will do that?"

He nodded. "She has connections everywhere. And right now we could really use them."

She smiled. "Lucky you." She turned and walked over to the bedroom window and stared out at the backyard. "It seems so odd to think that I knew my sister and then to find out I don't know anything about her."

"That's sad." He came up behind her, wrapped an arm around her shoulders, loving it when she turned and snuggled in close. They stood there at the window, looking out at the small empty grass yard, completely fenced, just like every other little cubicle along the strip. "You forget I was engaged to her, and apparently I didn't know anything about her either."

He could feel her head move slightly as she asked, "Do you ever think back on that time?"

"No. At the time I walked away, I just wanted to forget. I couldn't figure out how I'd made such a mistake, but then I figured she had to have been an active part of that mistake because obviously she didn't want to be with me."

"It sounds like she didn't know where she wanted to be."

"I think she wanted Jenny," Reyes said sincerely. "I don't think Reana knew how to make it happen without having the rest of her world implode."

They hung on to each other like that for several long moments. Then she whispered, "I'll be very grateful when this day ends."

He nodded. "It should have ended already. It's late, so let's stop our search for the moment to go see your mother. Then I'll drive you home."

She leaned back, looked up at him and smiled. "I forgot what a nice guy you are."

"*Shhh,*" he said with a wicked grin. "Don't tell the world that."

Her smile turned to a grin. "It's a myth that everybody wants a bad boy and that all the good guys are gone. Because a very good guy stands right in front of me."

His lips quirked. "Yeah? Then how come you never showed any interest in me?" he challenged. "Only your sister did."

"That's not true," Raina said with a laugh. "I was interested way before my sister. But, once she understood I liked you, she had to go after you. And, once you saw her in that light, you fell like a rock."

He stared down at her. "You said something like that before, but I didn't really believe you."

"It's true," she said, stepping out of his arms and moving a little farther back.

He let his arms drop. "Seriously?"

She tossed him an amused look. "Of course. Why would I lie about something like that? It was years ago."

He nodded thoughtfully. "And how do you feel about me now?"

She froze, turned to look at him and frowned. "You're not seriously bringing up something like that right now, are you? With everything else going on?"

"Why not?" he asked. "Because I liked you first. I assumed you didn't want anything to do with me."

Her jaw dropped. "How could you ever have gotten that assumption?"

"Because you never appeared to like me," he said.

She chuckled, and it soon turned into a great big laugh.

He stared at her in surprise but found his own sense of humor surfacing. "Or is this two quiet introverted people not really sure about how to come together?"

She giggled. "Absolutely. I kept looking at you sideways to the point that your mother chastised me for having a crush on you."

"Really?" He shook his head. "I never saw it. She never said anything about it. She actively pushed me toward Reana."

"Wow. I'd forgotten that," Raina agreed. "It seems like a long time ago in so many ways."

He thought back and nodded. "It has been years." He stopped and frowned. "You had a boyfriend back then."

"I had a *friend* back then," she corrected. "He was gay and was using me to get through life without other people questioning his sexuality," she said with a heavy sigh. "That's why I'm very saddened at my sister's inability to tell me about her own sexual orientation. I would never have judged

149

her. I would have been happy that she had finally figured it out. Because, from what I understand, coming to terms with it can be very traumatic for some people."

He turned and nodded and walked toward the door. "Come on. Let's go to the hospital—see if we can get one more thing checked off. And then you can get to bed."

"*Great*," she said. "Bed. Where I get to lie there and stare at the ceiling all night."

He tossed her a look. "Hopefully not tonight. It's been a very long day. You need sleep."

# Chapter 11

RAINA MIGHT NEED sleep, but she wouldn't get any; she knew that. Ice sent a text along their way to the hospital, saying the police weren't releasing the information on where her sister had died. Discouraged, Raina studied the hospital building on their approach. As they pulled into the parking lot, she stared up at the big building with a foreboding that wouldn't leave her alone.

"I don't want to go in there," she confessed.

"Why?" he asked as he pocketed the keys. He opened the door and stepped out, going around to her side. He opened the passenger door and helped her out. "Is something wrong, or are you just not sure how to handle your mother?"

"Who knows? Maybe I'm just too damn tired to sort any of it out." She looped her arm through his. "How long are you staying?"

"A couple days," he said. "Would you have dinner with me tomorrow night?"

She slid him a sideways look. "As old friends? Or is this a date?"

His lips quirked in that same old movement that had her heart hitching in response.

"How about both?" he asked. "Can't old friends go on a date?"

She chuckled. "Maybe. I'm not so sure what you'd call

that though."

"When you figure it out, tell me," he said lightly. "Because we'll probably spend all day together too. I just thought that we might share a nice meal too. Find out if we like each other—*really* like each other."

"In that case, yes," she said. "I'm not exactly sure how I feel about you at the moment."

It was his turn to raise his eyebrows.

"Sorry," she rushed to say. "I didn't mean that quite the way it sounded. I've always liked you, and you being here, with everything else going on, has my emotions in a mess."

"I'm not asking for any promises, but I would like to ask you to keep an open mind. At one point, we might have had the promise of something, until I allowed myself to be sidetracked by your sister."

"As did I," she said. "I'd like to think now that I'd fight for what I want, instead of letting my sister take over."

"And I'd like to think I would recognize true love, instead of allowing myself to be distracted by a shiny penny," he admitted. "And what I'd really like to do is spend more time with you." He squeezed her fingers and led the way to the front entrance.

Her heart melted a little more. This was why she'd really liked him in the first place. He was a whole lot of hero mixed with a very old-world gentlemanly charm. Something was almost innocent about him. It didn't match what she knew was the very capable man inside, but, when it came to relationships, there was a grace to him, a serenity. And she really liked that.

Inside the hospital, things were quiet. As they approached the floor where her mother was, it appeared to be visiting hours, as the noise grew louder the closer they got to the ward. As they entered her room, the room was empty of people, except for her mother.

Raina walked over to the bed and whispered, "Mom, it's me. Are you awake?"

Her mother opened her eyes and stared at her, hope in them at the sound of her voice, until hope faded as she realized it was the wrong sister.

Raina steeled herself against what she knew would be more pain, understanding there was just no way to get around it. Her mother would have to deal with the fact that she'd lost her favorite daughter.

Raina sat down beside her and said, "Reyes and I are both here."

Her mother narrowed her gaze as she studied Reyes. "Did you kill her?" she asked in a harsh whisper.

Reyes shook his head. "No, I did not." And then, almost as if he were tired of people accusing him of that, he asked in a forthright manner, "Did *you* kill her?"

Raina sucked in her breath. She watched her mother's face. First there was shock; then there was a realization, followed by tears.

"Why would you say that to me?" She squeezed her eyes shut for a long moment, then finally shook her head. "No," she said, "I didn't. I wouldn't. I just couldn't handle the news after Annemarie told me what had happened." She plucked nervously at the sheets and whispered, "I still can't."

"Why would the balcony be open in your room?" Raina asked. "I found you on your bed, but your window and the double glass doors were open. You never have those open."

Her mom looked at her, her bottom lip trembling.

Raina grasped her hand in hers. "It doesn't matter why that was. Just tell me, so I know. We've come up with all kinds of crazy scenarios—from an intruder to even Reana coming to see you."

Her mom shook her head. "Think about what I was trying to do and think about what's below my small balcony. I was looking out the window and realized the possibilities."

Raina thought for a moment and then said, "A patio is down there."

Her mom nodded. "I would have thrown myself over the edge of the railing."

Raina gasped. She couldn't imagine finding her mom's body broken on the patio. She shuddered, then mustered the courage to ask, "Why didn't you?"

"I was afraid it wouldn't do the job." Her mother's voice was broken and clogged with tears. "I was afraid I would just be more broken, more helpless afterward."

Raina bent over and kissed her mother's hand. "That's probably what would have happened because, while it looks like a long distance, I don't think the balcony would have been high enough from the patio to do more than maybe break a few bones."

"Exactly," she said. "And I wanted it to be complete." She stared around the hospital room. "And I failed in that too."

"Yes, you did," Raina said. "But this, this is about second chances."

Her mother's eyes filled with tears. "I get that. You know Reana and I had a special bond. Living without her is not something I want to do." Her voice was trident and clear.

Raina sat back, stared at their clasped hands and nodded. "I know you two shared something special, and I know you don't want to listen to me when I say, *This too shall pass*, and that you will feel better down the road when the grief is not quite so strong."

"No," her mother said. "Don't you understand? I don't want to forget. I don't want to get past this point. I don't want to go on. I loved your sister more than life itself. And to think of a day without her at my side is not something I want to struggle through." She started to sob again.

Raina looked at Reyes and shrugged. She didn't know what to do.

Reyes leaned down, patted her mother on the shoulder and said, "You might want to consider the fact that Raina has to make arrangements. Do you have any preference about what happens to Reana's body?"

At that, her mother's sobbing slowed. "You can't make those arrangements." The words came out in horror. "The police are still trying to figure out what happened."

"Yes, they are," Raina said. "But, as soon as they release the body, we need a plan in place."

"She wanted to be cremated," her mother whispered. "But I want her buried, so I can visit her grave."

"We can do both," Raina said. "We can get her cremated and still have a headstone and bury the ashes or do something where you have a memorial for her."

"No." Her mother's voice came out harder and louder. "I want her buried."

"Do you know if she has a will?" Reyes asked.

She stared at him, her gaze harder. "Why?" she snapped. "Do you think you're getting anything?"

"Mom, stop." Raina stepped in. "You don't have to be mean. He doesn't expect to get anything, but we have to take care of her estate, and that means we need to find her will."

Her mother seemed to collapse farther onto the bad.

"Whatever," she said. "Go do your thing. It's not like you give a damn about me anyway."

"I'm here, aren't I?" Raina tried hard to find a way to reach her mother. "I lost my sister too. It's not easy to deal with the loss and to help you to deal with yours."

"I never asked you to," her mother said, fatigue in her voice. "Just leave me alone. Make whatever arrangements you want to make."

As they turned to walk out of the room, her mother said, "Check her office at work. That's where she kept everything."

Back outside Reyes said, "Why have we not thought to check her office?"

"Because it's been a very long day," Raina said. "We also never figured out where she's been sleeping since Jenny moved out of the brownstone, though I'm pretty sure she moved back in with my mother for a few days." Raina glanced back at her mother's hospital room and decided she didn't want to ask her any more questions. "If that's the case, we should find her stuff at my mom's house. Another stop we have yet to make."

"Is her office still in the same place? Do you have keys?"

Raina nodded. "No, it's not the same place. She's got a different arrangement now. I don't know much about it. And no to keys."

"So, your mom's place first?"

She groaned. "I'm almost too tired to do anything," she said, "but, yes, we need to."

"I hate to say it, but the sooner, the better," Reyes said. "However, if you're that exhausted, you should go to bed. So let me take you home. I can go to your mom's house and to your sister's office."

"No," Raina said. "I don't want you going alone. It'll look suspicious as hell. And we don't want to do anything to bring the spotlight back on to you."

IT WAS NICE of her to always consider his position in this case. But she'd been going steady since early this morning, and it was now well past eleven. He wanted to take her back to her place, at least for a few hours.

As he sat in the Jeep, he stared at her, seeing her yawn. "I think I need to take you home instead of any more stops. At least for a few hours."

"Only if you go to bed too," she snapped with spirit. "And then we can both go to my mom's house in the morning. If we're up early enough, we can hit both places before it's time for the greenhouses to open."

At the thought of his own parents, he winced. "Good point."

She glanced at the time and gasped. "Can you return to Ice's father's place? Or do you want to stay at my place?"

"Do you have room?"

"I have a couch," she said with a half laugh. "I'm sure where you're currently staying is way more comfortable."

"Maybe," he said, "but it's not close, so potentially your place would be a better deal. At least then we can get up in the morning and take care of the rest of the things we have to check out."

"True," she said. "So, in that case, let's go to my place."

He followed her instructions until they got to her apartment building, and, as she directed him to the parking lot in the back, he realized the building itself was totally pitch dark.

"How long have you lived here?" he asked, frowning. "Why are there no lights? There should be outside security lights at the minimum."

"It's been like this for a few weeks. I've been here for a few years," she answered. "I moved in because it was cheap. Since then the management changed, and this one is much worse." She shrugged. "It's fine on a temporary basis. Personally I'd rather have land and live in a real home. But this works for now."

He smiled and nodded. "I hear you."

As they unlocked the door and walked into the apartment, he looked around with appreciation at how cozy and small it was. He eyed the couch and shrugged. "That'll work for now."

"Good," she grumbled, "because I'm too damn tired to fight over it. That's your bed if you want it. Otherwise you can go back to where you were staying before."

He chuckled. "Do you have a blanket and pillow?"

She stumbled into the bedroom and retrieved both items he'd asked for, plopped them on the couch and said, "I'm crashing." She threw her arms around him and gave him a hug. "Thank you for staying with me today."

"Hey, it was a shitty day. Nobody should be alone on a day like today."

She leaned back and smiled. "That's nice of you to say. Once again you're proving what a nice guy you are."

"Not sure I like being called a nice guy."

"You should," she said, "because you're one of them. And the world needs as many of those guys as we can get."

Then she turned and walked back into the bedroom and closed the door.

He looked at the couch, tossed the pillow at one end,

stretched out, pulled the blanket up to his shoulders and closed his eyes. He'd stayed overnight in a lot of crazy places, but, for right now, this was as good as it would get.

# Chapter 12

SOMEWHERE IN THE middle of the night she woke up with hot tears streaming down her face, heart-wrenching sobs racking her body, shaking the bed as grief overwhelmed her. Somewhere in her dreams the reality had set in, and it was pretty raw. It didn't matter that her sister was so young or that Reana no longer had the chance to live as she really should have. She was gone, and, like everybody else who dealt with loss, Raina could barely even begin this painful journey.

As the tears coursed down her face, she felt warm arms wrap around her. With a start, she remembered Reyes had slept on her couch. She turned to him for comfort, and he held her as she bawled, the grief ripping from her throat in great big waves of tears and noise.

He didn't say a word, just held her close, rubbed her back and let her cry. Once again proving he was one of those heroes of the world, one of the kind and compassionate men there for others in their time of need.

Somewhere along the line she drifted back to sleep.

Only to wake time and time again.

And always he was there.

Always he held her and let her cry.

"I need to forget," she whispered once.

"Sleep," he said, holding her close. "You need to sleep.

Let this drift away and stay away."

"I can't," she cried. "It hurts too much."

He stroked her tear-stained cheeks, her lips, brushing away the hot tears in her eyes. She bowed her head against his chest. "I feel so very alone."

"You're not alone," he whispered. "I'm here. I will be here for you."

"No." She shook her head. "No, you won't."

He placed a finger over her lips. "Yes, I will. I walked away from what we could have had a long time ago but not this time."

Her gaze widened as she understood what he said. She didn't want to believe it though. "Why did that happen back then? I so wanted to be with you."

"Because it needed to," he said quietly, his words heavy in the night. "We were different people back then. And maybe we both needed that time to become who we are now. And now we belong together," he said firmly.

She didn't dare believe him. She wanted to but didn't want to lose him again—not after so much loss in her life. "I couldn't stand to lose you again." She shuddered, feeling the same heavy emotions rack her spine.

"And you won't," he whispered, kissing her cheeks again.

She turned her head to meet his lips with her own. She slid her arms around his neck. "I want to believe ..."

"Then do," he murmured, gently kissing her again and again. "Just rest. Sleep. The world will be easier tomorrow. I'll still be here."

But it wasn't enough. She wanted so much more. An escape for one. She shifted so she leaned over him and reached down to kiss him fully on the lips, letting the passion she'd always kept reined in now have full freedom. If he meant those words, she wanted to find out now. If he was leaving, he needed to leave now by the same measure.

But his arms closed around her back, and he deepened the kiss with the same banked fires she held inside. Suddenly he rolled her onto her back and was atop her, holding his weight on his elbows but staring down at her.

She shook her head. "No more talking." And she pulled him down to her.

He lowered his head, and this time he held nothing back. His passionate kiss reached deep inside her and demanded a response.

The firestorm consumed them as they found each other. Mouths met and clung, tongues dueled gently, hands explored new territory, as they connected at the level they'd always craved and had never hoped to achieve.

She sighed happily, loving the weight of his body on hers, his hot skin sliding over hers. Their clothes had been quietly dispensed in the shadows as one piece followed another. Soft sighs of joy followed as more skin was revealed, until finally they were wrapped around each other, this time with her on top of him. She couldn't get enough of his heavily muscled body, the ridges of his ribs, his smooth flanks. She marveled at the well-made male in her arms. Even more so, that he was hers.

With a melting sigh, she stroked her hands across his chest, sliding down to the heavy ridge between his legs. Her fingers wrapped around him, sliding up and down, delighting as a heavy shudder racked his body. When she leaned over and kissed the tight head, he groaned. Then she slid her tongue across the slit at the top, and he flipped her onto her back and came down over her, her thighs pressed wide and him planted right where she wanted him.

Chuckling softly, she wrapped her thighs high on his hips and surged up against him.

"Witch," he whispered, his voice thick, hot.

And he plunged deep.

She cried out as he drove deep inside, then again and again. She matched his rhythm, then sped it up as need clawed through her. She was so close ...

He grabbed her hips and ground his pelvis against her, then drove hard and fast until she screamed his name—only to let out one raw aching sound of joy as her climax ripped through her. He gave an answering cry and surged once, then twice more before collapsing beside her.

Her breath let out in a deep gush, and she curled into him, content to let sleep finally take her under.

REYES HELD RAINA close as she succumbed to sleep. His heart still slammed against his ribs as he lay beside her, wondering at the vast shift in his world. A shift that had never felt more right.

She whimpered in his arms. He cuddled her close, fully prepared to stay awake all night, if that helped her sleep easy.

It hurt deeply to see her pain and to not be able to help. She didn't deserve this. She was such a sweetheart. Always had been.

She rolled over in his arms, sprawling across his chest, her bare leg across his thighs. He smiled, letting his hand gently stroke her smooth skin as she slept atop him.

His mind rolled with the puzzle pieces that weren't fitting together. They had to be missing something major here. No one committed murder without a good reason—at least to the murderer.

Her mother's suicide attempt at the same time just added to the shock and pain. He hurt for all involved, even himself. He'd known and loved Reana for a long time, but inside he just felt empty. He was sorry for her young life cut short, but his concern now was for her sister, the sleeping beauty in his arms.

To that end, he closed his eyes and rested.

He hoped they both got some sleep tonight because tomorrow, although a day later, would still be tough. For everyone.

# Chapter 13

W HEN SHE ROLLED over the next morning and opened her eyes, she could feel the sting of long dried tears. Her cheeks were tight and hot, her eyes caked with the saltiness left behind. Yet her body hummed with a replete satisfaction. She lay on her back for a long moment, his arms still wrapped around her. She cuddled in close, needing to know she wasn't alone. And hoping so very much that he would still be the Reyes she knew and loved in this morning after.

To know that Reyes understood, that he was in the same boat as her was huge. His capacity for understanding and compassion was something she hadn't seen in anyone else before. And she needed everything he had to give right now. She didn't even want to think about her mother. She'd always wanted to be a part of her mother's and sister's special relationship, and yet, had never been invited to join. Raina needed to find that same teenaged self-acceptance she'd found way back when, after she had first realized how that particular situation stood.

Indeed she didn't think she could. Just like the bond from birth between her and her sister, something even stronger existed between her sister and her mother. And, somewhere along the line, that bond between Raina and her sister had soured and had become almost a competition.

Only Reana had needed to win, and Raina hadn't cared.

She remembered what Jenny had said, and more waves of pain rose to the surface. Raina knew she'd be months dealing with this. It would be even more months before she could look back on her sister's life and not feel the same heartbreak she currently choked on.

She glanced at her cell phone and saw it was already almost eight o'clock. In spite of her emotional outburst in the night, and, likely because of Reyes's wonderful loving, she had slept.

She slipped from the covers and headed to the bathroom. Her face was puffy, her eyes red and bloodshot. She stepped into the shower and just stood with the heat of the water pouring down over her face. The puffiness probably needed cold water, but she didn't care. It just felt so good to feel everything wash away under the heavy water flow.

Finally she shut off the taps, wrapped herself in a towel and perched on the side of the bathtub. From where she sat, her world looked pretty miserable. But then so did her history, as she thought about how broken her relationship had been with her sister. So sad, particularly when they were twins.

Resolutely she got up, brushed her teeth and, grabbing her bathrobe, walked back out to the bedroom to find some clothes.

Reyes sat on the side of the bed. He studied her for a long moment, then stood and crossed the room to take her in arms and to cuddle her close. "How are you doing?"

She gave him a wan smile. "About as well as can be expected," she said softly. "Every day it will get better."

He nodded. "Did you leave me any hot water?"

Guiltily she whispered, "I'm not sure."

He gave a bark of laughter. "I'll find out." He kissed her gently, then walked into the bathroom.

She took the opportunity to find clean clothes, and, when she was dressed, she headed to the kitchen to put on coffee. She could hear him in the shower, so maybe he was either used to cold showers or she hadn't taken all the hot water.

Of all the days to not be considerate, this was probably one where she could get away with it. Which was too bad because he'd done so much for her.

With the coffee dripping, she opened the fridge, looking for food. They both needed to have a solid breakfast before they headed out. With any luck, today they'd get the answers they sought. Maybe with the truth, her mother could start to heal, and Raina's life and her mother's life could move on.

Just as she pulled out eggs and bacon, her phone rang. She glanced at it and saw it was the hospital. Her heart sinking, and with dread in her voice, she answered the call.

"I'm sorry to say," the doctor said, his voice calm and patient, "your mother had a cardiac arrest a few minutes ago. She didn't make it."

Raina didn't hear anything else. It was as if the world just spun into a crazy, out-of-control moment.

Reyes took her phone from her hand, turned her gently and pulled her in. She raised her arms instinctively around his neck. She was still frozen, still locked with disbelief.

He tilted her face up and said, "What was that?"

She just stared at him.

He looked down at the ID for the last caller and winced. "Your mother?"

"She had a heart attack this morning," she whispered, "and she didn't make it."

Reyes gave a strangled exclamation and pulled her tighter into his arms.

Her body had been warm but was now chilled; then it flushed with heat at the panic and rage. Why the rage, she had no idea. God, the pain ...

She had no more tears though, as if she had been completely emptied of them during the night. Dry-eyed, she sat down on the kitchen chair as he poured her a cup of coffee and placed it in front of her. She stared at it, then up at him. It was such a benign action, and yet, that little bit of normalcy helped pull her together.

"Did she have a heart condition?" he asked.

She looked at him once more and then slowly nodded. "Yes, she did. *Angina* I think they called it."

"Then maybe this isn't all that unexpected," he said quietly. "Devastating, shocking and, of course, painful. With that much more pain on top of your already horrible loss but maybe not so unexpected."

She stared at him. "All I can think of is that she is happy now. She gets to be with Reana."

And, with those words, raw ugly sobs ripped from her throat. She couldn't believe it. She shouldn't have had any more crying left to do. There shouldn't have been any more sobs or tears left to shed. But apparently this raw ugly truth was just a little more than she could handle.

Once again he wrapped her up in his arms and held her.

When the crying jag was finally over, and she lay curled up on his lap, sharing a chair at the kitchen table, she whispered, "You're good at that."

He leaned over and kissed her temple. "I haven't had much experience with it," he said. "After hearing you for the last twenty-four hours ... To see someone in so much pain and to know there's nothing you can do to help …"

"What you're doing is helping." She got up, reached for the Kleenex on the counter and blew her nose. Then she wiped her eyes and sat down on the chair in front of her coffee. "I'll focus on the fact my mother has what she wanted," she said resolutely.

She knew more grief would come, more sadness for what could have been, more loss down the road when the little things would hit her, but she also understood in her heart of hearts that this was what her mother had truly wished for.

She stared at him and said, "I don't have any right to ask this of you …"

He grabbed her hand and said, "Ask anyway."

She gave him a small smile. "Any chance you can delay going home for a couple days until I can get them both buried?"

He nodded. "Absolutely. You shouldn't be alone right now."

"It's not so much about being alone," she whispered, "I'm being selfish. I want somebody to help me, somebody to stand there beside me at their graves. I'm not sure what to do at this point." She stared blindly around the apartment. "My mother wanted Reana buried, so Mom would have a place to visit, but I know my sister wanted to be cremated."

"What did your mother want for herself?" he asked.

She stared at him in surprise. "Cremated. It was always to be cremations. She wanted her ashes planted in a garden or thrown out in the ocean."

"Then we'll do that," he said firmly. "We'll find a place, take both of them, and we'll put them back into Mother Nature where they came from."

She smiled. "She'd like that. She loved plants. In a way,

she was jealous of the work I did because she didn't have a green thumb but had always wanted to be involved in the business."

"I didn't know that," he said in surprise. "Did she ever talk to Annemarie about her desire? Maybe that would have been a place for her."

"I have no clue." Raina lifted her cup of coffee and stared at the black liquid. Then it hit her. "I'm an orphan now. I have no family, no aunts, no uncles, no siblings." She stared at him in surprise. "To a certain extent, I always felt that way because the two of them were so close, and I was the third wheel who didn't fit, but they were always there, always a part of my life. They were still family."

"And this too shall pass," he said gently. "They will take their place in your memory as you move forward. What you can't do is let them stop you from living a full life."

Her smile turned sad. "No, I won't do that. But it feels very strange right now."

"Lonely?" he asked.

"Well, it would be," she said, "but you're here. And I don't want to impose or expect more from a friendship than I should."

"Stop," he interrupted. "We've been friends for a long time. We're something more now. I'm just not sure what."

She smiled, liking the thought. Then she realized he was right. "We have always been on that edge, haven't we?"

He nodded. "Even when I took that wrong turn, we were still on that edge. Did I tell you how much relief was in my heart after I found out about Reana's affair? I'd gone there to break up with her because I couldn't stand it anymore. Everything felt wrong. I didn't want to see her anymore. I didn't want to be with her. I didn't want to make plans with her. I just wanted her out of my life. And every time I thought about moving forward, it was always with you," he said. "I didn't know how to make the switch from one to the other without it seeming like I was replacing her with you."

Stunned, she stared at him. "I must have thought that myself."

He nodded. "When I left, I planned on coming back long before now. I planned on getting in contact to see what you were up to, whether something was still between us."

"Two years is a long time to leave it," she said drily.

He nodded. "Guilty as charged. I got buried in the work I was in, and I did that deliberately so I could heal. It was not peaceful being in a relationship with Reana. I felt torn, twisted up sometimes, shocked about some of the things she said and did. It wasn't an easy relationship by any means."

Raina nodded. "I do understand. I loved her dearly, but she was in a self-destructive mode, and, if she wasn't self-destructing, she was destroying others."

He smiled. "Let's get breakfast, follow up with the things we planned to do yesterday, then we have some funeral arrangements to make."

She gave him a sad smile. "Agreed." She glanced at the bacon and eggs, still on the countertop. "So who'll cook? You or me?"

He chuckled. "How about me?"

REYES GOT UP after finishing his plate of food. He'd been watching her carefully to see if she would eat. She seemed to pick up a new wind of energy. He knew the grief was just being put aside to deal with later. That was the way it should be. There was only so much one could handle at once. First her sister and then her mother. Although Raina appeared to be more at peace about her mother, it was still a lot of changes for her.

They had to see if they could do anything to clear up the mystery about her sister's murder. Then they had two funerals to arrange. He thought about the pain involved in something like that and shook his head.

He quickly washed up the few dishes.

Behind him, she said, "You do realize we have a dishwasher, right?"

He turned around to look at her and smiled. "Sure, but it's just the two of us, and we don't have much in the way of dishes." He watched her grab a notepad and a pen. "What are you writing down?"

"I'm getting rid of all the things in my head that need to be done," she said. "There are a lot of notifications, not to mention all we were planning today."

"Now we have to look at your mom's house in a different light," he said. "So I suggest we start there."

"What are we looking for?"

He hesitated as he grabbed a tea towel to dry his hands. "Well, to start with, we need wills." He watched as her hand froze above the notepad; then slowly she wrote down a list of what they were looking for. "We also need to see if any of your sister's belongings are at your mother's, and we have to go to Reana's office too."

Raina nodded and kept writing. He wanted to walk over and see what she'd put down, but it almost seemed intrusive. He took the tea towel and wiped off the table and refilled her coffee cup.

"When you're done with your coffee," he said, "I suggest

we leave. We'll have to contact quite a few people. I don't know if you have the phone numbers of those we need to call."

She shook her head. "No, not really. I'll find them at Mom's house. She had an address book."

"And we need to get into their computers," he said.

She winced. "That we do. I'll check out my mom's emails, let her old boyfriend know she won't make their coffee date. And we have to post on her social media."

He winced at that. It wasn't something he was good at. Social media was for other people. He tended to be much more private and didn't spend his time posting things about his day for others to see. But he knew half the world completely disagreed with him on that.

She snatched her pad of paper, walked to the closet, grabbed a purse bigger than her normal one, stuffed the pad inside, went to her regular purse, pulled out her wallet and keys, added her cell phone, then disappeared into her bedroom.

When she reappeared with a sweater draped over her arm, he nodded and said, "Ready?"

She smiled. "As ready as I'll ever be. Yesterday I thought one day could not get any worse ..."

"It doesn't mean today is any worse," he said quietly. "You know what she did yesterday. You know how much she wanted to be with your sister. If she pined away, and her heart gave out for that reason, it's pretty hard to argue with."

She smiled. "It's much easier to deal with a natural death than a murder."

On that note they walked out of the apartment and headed for his Jeep.

# Chapter 14

"I T'LL BE A long day," she said as they pulled up to her mother's house.

"Did your mom own the house?"

She nodded. "Yes. And it was paid for. She had life insurance from my father's death."

"Well, that's good," he said in surprise.

"It's good, but she didn't have enough to live on her own, even without that expense. That's why she worked part-time, even though she shouldn't have had to."

"Just because we want to be in a position where we don't have to work," he said, "doesn't mean we are always so lucky."

"I know," she said. "She's lucky to have been as well off as she was."

They walked in the front door, and Raina stood in the hallway.

"I hate to ask," he said, "but do you know how her assets are to be divided?"

She shot him a look. "Equally between the two of us. But, until I have a will in hand, I won't really know."

"Do you think she has one?"

"I believe so. My sister was always big on that." At the frown on his face, she looked at him and shrugged. "Yes, it's possible my sister did something so that everything went to her. I can't say one way or the other. If it's that way, I'll deal with it. I've had enough of that behavior from Reana all my life. It would hardly be a shock."

He gave a hard look. "Still doesn't make it right."

"No, it doesn't," she whispered. She headed toward the living room. "Let's start in here."

They took a quick glance around, but, outside of a coffee table with a drawer, there wasn't a lot to look through. Then they headed to the kitchen and dining room.

"Your mom wasn't much of a hoarder, was she?"

"No, she wasn't at all. She didn't have money for knick-knacks, and, after my father's death, instead of hanging on to things, she got rid of everything. She said it was much easier to deal with than to see him in every bit and piece he had left in the house."

"That's an unusual reaction."

"Maybe," she said, "but that was Mom. She did things her way. It didn't matter if you agreed or not."

"Maybe it'll make it easier for you to clean up the house before selling it or renting it or whatever." He glanced around the living room, overstuffed with furniture and the large older dining room set. "I don't think any of this is worth much money, but maybe it has sentimental value for you."

"That's not really who I am either," she said, fatigue in her voice. "But thankfully I don't have to make decisions on that stuff yet."

After the living room and dining room, they went toward the kitchen. She stood in the front hall again, checking out the closet, just because it was there.

"Nothing of Reana's appears to be here. Maybe it's all up in the guest bedroom, not the small bedroom we were in yesterday, but the bigger bedroom on the opposite end of the hallway from Mom's bedroom."

They made their way upstairs to the three bedrooms.

"It's a small house," he said, "but your mom didn't need more than this, living alone."

They walked into the master bedroom, and Raina froze. Once again, he lay a hand on her shoulder. She tilted her head to rest on top of it and whispered, "This is hard."

"Of course it is," he said. A large chair was off to the side. He brought it over and helped her to it. "Just sit. Her laptop is on the night table. I'll grab it for you." He picked it up and brought it to her.

She turned it on while he went through the night table drawers. He looked around and said, "Did she have a safety deposit box?"

"No, she kept everything in the bottom drawer of the dresser, as far as I know."

He headed to the dresser and went systematically from the top drawer down. When he hit the bottom drawer, he pulled out 9x13 envelopes of paperwork. "This looks to be legal stuff. She has a file from a lawyer's office."

"That's probably the one addressing her estate," she said absentmindedly as she flicked through her mother's emails. Nothing appeared startling. "What's the lawyer's name?"

"Macaulay and Sons," he said.

She typed that into the search bar of the emails and brought a few up. "Mom redid her will a year ago," she said and read quickly through the emails. She glanced up. "I wonder why she did that?"

He just watched her.

She frowned, feeling her stomach twist. "Yes, it's possible," she said, and then, more as a mantra for herself, she added, "Again I will deal with it, if that's what it is."

He handed her the envelopes. "I suggest you start with calling the lawyer."

Surprised, but realizing the sense of his suggestion, she pulled out her phone and dialed the office. When the secretary answered, she asked to speak to Larry Macaulay.

"What's this regarding?"

"My mother," Raina said. "Melissa Woodcroft passed away this morning."

"Oh, I'm so sorry," the secretary said. "Hang on a moment. I'll get him for you." Then she stopped and asked, "Who is calling please?"

"It's one of her twin daughters, Raina."

"Thank you."

Within a few seconds a man's voice came on the phone. "Raina?"

"Yes," she said. "I'm Melissa Woodcroft's daughter."

"Yes," he said. "And what's this that I hear about your mother?"

"The hospital called me this morning," she said. "Apparently she had a heart attack and passed away. I'm on my way to the hospital soon. I just thought I should let you know."

"Absolutely," he said. "We have her will and will handle her estate here."

"Do you also handle my sister's estate?" she asked, finding it difficult to get the question out.

"Reana's? Yes, of course," he said. "I think you're the only one who hasn't been into the office."

"I'm the only one who doesn't have any estate to handle," she said half humorously. And then she remembered who she was talking to and why. "I don't know if you've heard, but my sister was found murdered yesterday."

Dead silence followed on the end of the phone. "What?"

"Yes," she said. "In effect, I just became an orphan." And her voice choked on that word.

"Oh, my dear," he whispered. "I am so sorry. Rest assured we'll get everything handled on our end, but I need you to come in to the office."

"Yes, of course," she said. "Can you contact the hospital for the death certificates? Or is that something I need to do?"

"Let me look into it. If we can do it, then, of course, we'll do it without bothering you. Do the police have any idea what happened?" he asked, his voice diffident and hesitant.

"No," she said. "They're still investigating."

"That makes it very difficult for you. To lose both your sister and your mother."

"Well, you might as well understand the whole story," she said. "When my sister was murdered, my mother tried to commit suicide. It was just too much for her heart, and early this morning she had a heart attack."

His gasping horror came through the speaker, and his voice warmed up several degrees. "I am so sorry, Raina. I know we've never met, and these certainly aren't the circumstances under which I would choose to meet you, but, if there's anything we can do to make it easier on you, please let us know."

"That's why I'm calling," she said. "I'm at Mom's house right now. We found a bunch of legal paperwork in the bottom of her dresser. I just didn't know what I was supposed to do next."

"Whenever the bodies are released," he said, "funeral arrangements will need to be made."

"Is that information you have as well?" she asked. "As far

as I know, they both wanted to be cremated."

"That's my understanding, but I will pull both files and take a closer look," he said. "I'll get back to you on that."

"Okay," she said, relief in her voice. "And I don't really know how to handle their estates."

"That's why we're here," he said with forced cheer. "Let me check on the files. I'll call the hospital, then I'll get back to you."

"That's fine," she said. She hung up and looked at Reyes. "Apparently they'll be handling both my sister's and my mother's estates."

"Your sister had money?"

"She had the brownstone," Raina said. "I don't even own my apartment. I just bank my money and pay rent."

"Why is that?" he asked.

"I don't know." She shrugged. "I never felt like this was home. I never saw a place I wanted enough to lock myself into ownership, and I guess I always thought that maybe something would happen, and I would need to move." She frowned, not even sure what she meant by that. "I don't know. I guess it just didn't feel right."

He nodded. "A bunch of other paperwork is here. Some photocopies of your birth certificates, things like that."

She glanced at him and sighed. "I probably need all that." She stood, walked to her mother's closet. Inside was a large empty beach bag. She held it out to him. "Can you pack up all the paperwork for me?"

He did that, and she added her mother's laptop. Raina turned, looked around, then back at him. "I don't really want to stay here."

He nodded, glanced into the spare bedroom and the guest bedroom, and led the way back downstairs and outside.

"Next we have to go to my sister's office," she said. "Her list of clients have to be contacted. I don't even know how her business can transfer over to someone else or what happens to all the records."

"Hopefully the lawyer can handle that too," Reyes said. "Come on. Let's go there now."

It was about fifteen minutes to her sister's small office. He pulled into a parking space, and they walked in, surprised to find a receptionist out front.

The woman looked up and smiled. "Well, you definitely look like your sister."

Raina nodded. "I'm Raina and this is Reyes." She asked, "Do you work for her?"

"Partially," she said. "We have several accountants here. I work for all of them."

With relief Raina realized maybe her sister's business wouldn't be quite such a headache. "Are the other accountants here?"

The receptionist nodded cheerfully. "Yep, everybody is in, working hard."

"Is it possible to speak to them all at once?"

Something in her voice must have alerted the receptionist that the meeting wouldn't be pleasant. She looked from Raina to Reyes, swallowed hard and said, "I can bring them out here."

"Please do that." As the woman got up, Reyes asked, "Who all works here?"

She pointed to the row of business cards on her desk. "There are four accountants. Reana is one of them."

"Interesting," Reyes said. He picked up the business cards of the others. And, for good measure, grabbed one of Reana's.

"Who are you?" the receptionist asked.

He gave a humorous glance. "Her ex-fiancé. But that was two years ago."

The woman stared at him.

Raina's words nudged her. "If you wouldn't mind gathering the others? Then we need to go to her office."

The receptionist fled.

They could hear voices and doors opening and closing. Within a few minutes the other accountants came out.

Raina studied them, but not one of them looked like a murderer. Then again, she didn't know what a murderer looked like. They were all geeky, wearing glasses, and much older than Reana. As they came out, they looked at her curiously.

"What's this all about?" asked the oldest. He had to be at least sixty, maybe sixty-five.

"It's about my sister, Reana," Raina said quietly. "She was murdered."

A horrified gasp circulated among the three accountants and their receptionist. "What?" one of the men asked. "When?"

Raina took a deep breath. "Yesterday morning. I'm sorry. I should have been here yesterday, but I was caught up in things."

One of the men harrumphed. "Well, it would have been nice if you'd caught up with us."

Reyes stepped forward, his hand going to Raina's shoulder. "Before you judge her for not having been here immediately, you need to understand what she was dealing with. Her mother tried to commit suicide yesterday morning, after finding out about Reana, and has since died of a heart attack this morning. Raina's dealing with the loss of both her sister and her mother right now. And her plate is rather full."

The man stepped back, shamefaced. "I'm so sorry," he whispered, shaking his head. "This is just terrible."

"We've contacted the lawyer this morning regarding Reana's estate," he said. "But we have no clue what's to happen to the business side of it."

"We do have provisions in place," the same man said. "We'll split up her clients, contact them individually, ask if they want to transfer to one of us. If not, they're free to take their business elsewhere. But we'll have to see what she has in progress."

"What kind of bookkeeping and accounting did she do?"

"Small business and personal," he said. "Nothing major. Nothing that would get her murdered, if that's what you're asking." He glanced around, "I presume we'll have the police here then to?"

"I texted them this morning," Reyes explained, "saying we were coming here. So chances are they'll be here sometime today, yes."

She hadn't realized he'd done that, but it figured. It was best to keep the police in the loop as they made every step.

"May I see my sister's office please?" she asked.

They frowned and looked at each other.

"All the material in there is confidential."

"Well, some of it is, but some of it is personal. And we're trying to sort through her private life, so we can deal with those issues too."

The receptionist said, "I can show you what's hers."

Reyes nodded. "We'd appreciate that. The police will presumably go through what they need to," he said, his voice harder.

The men all nodded. "We'll be as cooperative as we can be."

"Can you tell us how she died?" one of the accountants asked.

"She was beaten and then shot," Raina said, her voice getting fainter as she repeated the words that hurt so much. "Her body was found yesterday morning."

"Was she murdered at home?" one of the men asked.

Reyes turned to look at him. "We only know that she was found in her vehicle." He studied the men. "Do you have anybody in mind who might have murdered her?" he asked in a slightly challenging voice.

All the men stiffened.

"We're all family men. None of us were involved with her on a personal level, if that's what you're talking about," one of the men said. "Not only that, we have a business relationship with her, and there's been no strife."

"If she was found in her vehicle, it could be a stranger," another one said.

"If it was just a gunshot, then maybe," Reyes said quietly. "But the beating..." He shook his head. "No, that's personal."

The men took several long, deep breaths, as if scared to say the wrong thing.

Reyes glanced at the receptionist. "Do you mind?"

She nodded and hurried toward the first door on the left.

As they stepped in, Raina was filled with a wash of memories and homesickness. On the back counter was a picture of her and her sister. Raina walked around the desk and picked it up. It brought tears to her eyes. "I'm not even sure when this was taken," she said. "And I had no idea she kept it."

"She's had it here since she first started," said one of the men.

Raina turned to see all three men jammed into the small office. She wasn't sure if they wanted to be sure nothing implicated them. She glanced around to see her sister's long flowing maxivest hanging on the hook on the door. Her heart slowed, then raced as she recognized her sister's favorite sweater. She wore it all the time. Just to know it would never wrap around her sister's shoulders made her heart ache.

"I'll get you a box for her personal items," one of the men said. He disappeared out the door and around the corner.

Raina sat down at the desk, reached for a Kleenex and blew her nose. "I'm sorry. It's been a very difficult two days."

"You've got nothing to be sorry about. Reana will be missed," the older of the men said. "She was very good with the clients."

"Was she?" Reyes asked. "It seems like she was a different person to each of us."

"Yes, I would agree with that entirely. Sometimes she was very calm and peaceful. And other times she was almost hardened."

"Yes," the receptionist said. "But she was usually very nice."

Raina registered the word *usually*. But then the receptionist was also pretty and young, and Reana didn't like competition, so Raina understood that not everything might have gone smoothly. She opened Reana's drawers, looking for anything personal that needed to be removed, finding a lot of pens and pencils, pads of paper. At the back was an address book. She pulled it out, flipping through it. It opened automatically to Jenny's name. There was Jenny's number and beside it was her brother, Jamie's, number, reminding Raina that they hadn't heard back from him. She shuffled through the rest and found several more names, but they were mostly scratched out. Raina could almost safely assume they were all Reana's boyfriends at one time or another.

That was her sister; Reana dove in, and then she abruptly stepped out. And, when she was done, she was done. But apparently not with Jenny. Just more proof that Jenny had really mattered.

Raina was emotional by the time Reyes picked up the box they had packed. She thanked the others. "If you think of anybody who might have wanted to hurt her, a disgruntled client, somebody, a friend who might have come here at any time, please, *please* let us know."

The men all nodded.

They left a sad trio of accountants behind as they walked out the door. They headed toward the Jeep, and Raina blew her nose again, carrying a handful of Kleenex with her all the time now.

As they sat in the Jeep, Reyes asked, "What do you think?"

"I think she was a bright light for all of them. And I think, when they went home, they went home to families, to wives and children, but, when they came back again, Reana was someone they looked forward to seeing every day. It will be a loss for them all."

"Do you think any of them could have killed her?" He started up the engine.

She shook her head. "I didn't get those vibes. But then again, what do I know? I've never seen a murderer before."

"Unfortunately they can look exactly the same as you and me."

"I DO WANT to contact Jamie," Reyes said.

"He still hasn't called, has he?"

"No," he said. He glanced at his watch. "A phone message probably won't be heard until the receptionist shows up, won't become a priority until then."

"True enough," she said. "Now we've collected a boxful of sadness, but we didn't check to see if my sister was staying at my mom's house."

"She was," he said. "I saw suitcases in the guest bedroom."

"When did you look?"

"Initially when you were on the laptop," he said. "The bed had been slept in but was made. The suitcases were in the closet at the back. They do appear to be filled with her clothes."

"I don't know if she'd been there the last night or not, and of course, we can't ask my mother anymore," she whispered.

"Exactly. I suspect Reana was meeting someone, and that person was the last one to see her alive."

"Right." She pulled out her sister's address book. "I kept this out of the box," she said. "Do you want to call Jamie?"

Just then Reyes's phone rang. He pulled off to the side of the road. It was one of the detectives. He talked to Detective Burgess, filling him in on what they'd found at Reana's place of work, then told him about her mother.

"The autopsy has been completed," Detective Burgess said.

"When can the body be released?" Reyes asked.

"Not yet," the detective said. "It will probably be another day or two."

"Raina wants to hold a service for the two of them together," he said. "So please, let's not have it take too long."

"I'll do my best. We still haven't found any leads. No fingerprints were on or in the vehicle, and, though we have ballistics from the gun, we don't have any matching results back yet."

"We only have one more person left to contact," Reyes said. "Jenny's brother."

"Do you have his number?"

Reyes held out his hand for the address book and read off Jamie's number. "I contacted him at the end of the day yesterday. If nothing else, I'd just like to confirm that Jenny did move out as she told us."

"We'll give him a call right now," the detective said. "We'd like to talk to him before you two do."

"Okay," Reyes said. "We now have a service for two to arrange, two estates to handle. That's why I need the bodies released." He gave the detective the lawyer's name and phone number as well. "In case you have any questions about the estate, we don't have any answers. But the attorney should give you some."

"That would be good," the detective said. "It'll help us tick off a few boxes."

"Exactly. I don't think Reana's murder was for money. At this point, all I can see was passion."

"A disgruntled boyfriend?"

"Or a disgruntled girlfriend," Reyes said. "Reana loved Jenny, but that doesn't mean, while she was in the middle of a breakup, she didn't have an affair with somebody else."

"No," the detective said. "And, considering they didn't steal the car or her purse inside the car, that lends some credence to the murder not being about a burglary."

"I would say it's definitely personal. I'm sure you agree."

The detective sighed. "That's the way we're leaning."

"But we're not having much luck running down too many of her friends."

"We did find a couple ex-boyfriends through your mother's business. Apparently Reana dated some of the men who worked there. But they didn't have much to say. Except to say it was short, sometimes sweet and sometimes not. But their relationships were all over a long time ago. ... They all said she seemed sad when she was with them."

"We're back to that twisted-up-on-the-inside thing," Reyes said. After signing off, he turned to look at Raina. "Not a whole lot new." He explained the little bit they found out.

She nodded. "It will be somebody who lost his temper," she whispered. "My sister was good at spiking tempers."

Reyes had to agree. She'd pricked his all the time. The thing was, he'd taken a long time to boil and had very good control even then. But lots of people didn't. "Doesn't the gun add a different element?" he asked, thinking about it.

"I can see, after beating her up, how he'd decide that he'd have to kill her before she woke up and called the cops."

"The detective is calling Jamie right now," he said.

"That would be good," she said. "Even if only to confirm Jenny's story."

"Do you feel any differently about Jenny?"

"No," Raina said. "I don't think she did it."

"Why is that?"

"Because she loved Reana. Like she *really*, really loved

her. I think my sister was a fool to have lost that. Sometimes that kind of love only happens once in a lifetime."

"I can see that." He couldn't argue with that. He had hopes himself of getting his love life back on the right track too. Especially now that he'd found Raina again.

# Chapter 15

S OMETHING WAS IN his voice. Raina glanced at Reyes. "Are you saying you really loved her, and then you lost her?" she asked curiously.

He shook his head. "No. I don't think I ever really loved her. And I don't think she ever really loved me. But, of course, it's not that easy to know at this point." He seemed to hesitate, then motioned at her list. "Where to now?"

"I feel like I'm supposed to see my mother, but she's gone, so I don't know what I'm supposed to do there."

"Maybe you want to say goodbye," he said. "We could go to the morgue and see her."

She thought about it, then shook her head. "No, I don't feel like that's something I need to do."

"Fine," he said. "Maybe we should talk to Jamie. If nothing else, he's the last person on our list. With any luck the police have already spoken to him, so we won't be stepping on any toes."

"There're all these boyfriends in her address book with their names crossed off."

"But we don't have the last names for a lot of them, and we don't know who the police have already contacted. I suggest we talk to Jamie, if he'll even see us," he added. "Then we'll stop off at the police station, hand over the address book, and see if the detective can confirm anything.

Then I really want to stop in at my mother's, if you wouldn't mind going to the greenhouses."

"Oh my gosh," she cried out. "I forgot about your family." She glanced at her watch. "Why don't we go there first? The police might need more time to talk to Jamie anyway."

Reyes thought about it and nodded. "My family probably wants an update. Beside we haven't told my mother about your mother."

"Oh, Lord," Raina whispered. "I'm not looking forward to telling her. It's just way too sad."

He nodded and drove on steadily.

"Your mom will blame herself, won't she?"

He shrugged. "I'm not sure, but she should," he said. "I know that sounds harsh, but she really had no business speaking to your mom like that."

"They were friends though," Raina said. "Maybe it does make *some* sense."

"It's too late to worry about it now," he said. They pulled up outside of the busy greenhouses and parked. He looked at the vehicles lining the parking lot. "The business is doing really well, isn't it?"

"Yes, it is," she said. She hopped out, tucked the address book into her pocket and walked forward. Several of the staff members called out to her. She lifted a hand and waved but didn't say much. With Reyes at her side, she headed toward Annemarie's office.

Raised voices could be heard on the other side of the closed door. She glanced at Reyes.

He sighed, squared his shoulders and said, "My parents never stop arguing, do they?"

She shook her head. "No, they really don't." She knocked on the door.

The voices silenced. Harold called out, "Come in."

She pushed open the door and stepped inside with Reyes behind her. Both Annemarie and Harold looked at them, smiles breaking out and Annemarie racing to Raina. "Oh, my dear. I'm so sorry about your sister."

"Mom, it's worse than that."

Annemarie stiffened and frowned at her son. "What are you talking about?"

"Melissa tried to commit suicide yesterday morning, as you already know. But she had a heart attack early this morning, and she didn't make it."

Annemarie cried out, her hands instinctively reaching for her husband. He wrapped her up and held her tight. They both studied Reyes.

"You don't blame me for this, do you?" his mother cried out.

Reyes didn't say anything right away. He turned to look at Raina.

She sighed, shoved her hands in her pockets and said, "I'll never really know the truth, will I? If you hadn't called her, would my mother still be alive? I had planned to tell her and to stay with her, once I confirmed it truly was Reana's body in the morgue. Would Mom had have taken this step if she hadn't been alone? Or would she have just waited and tried to commit suicide later? I won't ever know."

Annemarie cried out again. Raina felt sad, but it was the truth. "I am upset you called her, as if to share the latest gossip. I'm pretty sure her heart attack was brought on by her attempted suicide. It's easy to say it was a broken heart, and she just wanted to join my sister," she said. "But I will always wonder, if she'd had someone with her, would she still be alive?"

Annemarie started to cry. "I didn't mean to hurt her," she sobbed.

Harold glared at the two of them. "You can't seriously think Annemarie's responsible for your mother's death?"

"No," Raina said quietly. "But I certainly think that the way Annemarie jumped into telling Melissa—and then didn't make sure she was okay afterward—definitely contributed to it." She stared at Harold. "Am I blaming her? No. Right now I'm still angry, still hurt, and still very confused," she said quietly. "I now have two family members to say goodbye to. And one is hard enough."

On that note she turned and walked back out again.

REYES TURNED TO face his father. "It's been a very difficult time for Raina," he said by way of explanation. "First her sister and now her mother."

Annemarie rubbed her eyes. "You know I'd never have done anything like that on purpose."

"No," Reyes said. "I don't think you called her to let her know her daughter was dead, thinking she'd try to commit suicide and then would have a heart attack. But I do think you wanted to be in the middle of something once again." He knew his words hurt, but he had to tell her the truth. "You had no business informing Melissa. And when you did inform her, you did absolutely nothing to make sure that broken woman was okay. Obviously somebody should have been there with her. And that was Raina's place to be. And you took that from her. I think, from Raina's point of view, that'll be very hard to reconcile."

Annemarie sat down slowly in her chair. She grabbed several Kleenexes and wiped her face. "It's something I'll have to live with too," she said painfully. "I know right now it doesn't matter to you, but Melissa was my friend too."

"Yes, she was," Reyes said. "And now she's gone from both of your lives." He glanced back to see Raina standing at the corner of the shop, looking out the window at the plants. "And I'm sure you can see how very confusing and trying this is for Raina."

Harold stepped forward. "When are you leaving?"

"Meaning, that I've been here long enough to cause all kinds of hell?" Reyes asked humorously, trying not to take offense, but, in a way, it was hard not to.

His father had the grace to turn red. "That's not what I mean," he blustered.

"Well, it is, just you aren't usually so blunt," Reyes said drily. "I'm staying for Raina's sake because she asked me to," he said quietly. "Until the joint memorial service is over."

Harold winced. He glanced at Raina. "That will help her."

"Yes," Reyes said. "At least I hope it will. The other thing that will help is to make sure we find out who killed her sister."

He turned to face his mother. "Did Reana ever have any of her friends stop by?"

"I gave the police a list of anybody I knew," she said. She rubbed her face. "God, this has been a terrible couple days." She caught Reyes's look and flushed. "I cared a lot about Reana," she said. "And her mother was a good friend of mine. These deaths will affect us regardless of what you think of me."

"I don't think badly of you," he said quietly. "But, like Reana, you're all about drama. You're all about getting into things that you really don't have any right to be in."

She stiffened and glared at him. His father stepped forward, and then she burst into tears and said, "No, you're right. You're very right, and I'm so sorry."

Harold looked from her to Reyes and shrugged.

Reyes understood his father's position. It was how Reyes felt around his mother too. "Well, hopefully this has been a lesson for everyone," Reyes said quietly. "And I'm here to tell you that, if I get a chance"—he turned to check where Raina was, seeing her out in the store—"I'll convince Raina to move to Texas with me. That will be easier for both of you."

Her mother gasped. "Are you two together?"

He tilted his head to the side. "Would it bother you if we are?"

She shook her head. "No. It's a much better pairing than you and Reana. I understand that now."

"Yes. It always was Raina for me," he said quietly. "Things got off track for a while there. But it's slowly going back in the right direction."

"She probably doesn't want to work here anymore either," Annemarie said with a sad smile. "I've broken something between us."

Reyes didn't know what to say to his mother about that. Communication was strained when he had such a difficult parent. In all the time he'd spent with friends and coworkers, they had never seemed to have anybody in their lives like his mother. He loved her, but she wasn't easy to live with.

"Since I haven't discussed this with Raina yet, I don't know what she wants to do right now," he said. "It's too early for her to make those decisions. For now she's got a hell of a mess to deal with."

His mother nodded, her hands clenched on the table in front of her. "Also some rumors are circulating," she said slowly, "about Reana having girlfriends. Is that true?"

He nodded. "It's why she and I broke up," he said. "I found her in bed with her girlfriend."

Both his parents gasped. "Why didn't you tell us?" Harold asked, a bit confused. "We listened to what she said and believed her."

"Of course you did," he said drily. "Everybody believed everything Reana said."

His mom just stared at him, as she lurched to her feet. "All these years I thought it was because of you. Why did she slap you when you first arrived then?" she asked in confusion.

"I think she was afraid I might tell everyone the truth," he said tiredly. "Now that she's gone, it doesn't matter anyway." Reyes studied his mother's face. "The thing is, you never believed me. You've *always* believed her."

His mother once again sat down heavily. She looked like she was about to break apart.

He took a step toward her, his instincts aroused. "What's going on?"

"I saw her," she whispered. "The night she died."

His father turned to look at her. "What?"

She raised tear-filled eyes toward both men. "I didn't kill her though. Please believe me. I did not kill her."

"What happened?" Reyes asked. He was aware of Raina stepping up behind him; she'd been close enough to hear this most recent part of their conversation.

"I asked her why she caused the scene with you. I didn't want her picking on you anymore."

Reyes was surprised at the warmth that spread through him. His mother had never been terribly good at defending him. "Why this time?" he asked curiously.

She flushed. "Because I figured, after two years, you deserved another chance."

"With her?" he asked incredulously. "I had no intention of ever getting back together with her, if that's what you're thinking."

"She'd been saying some pretty rough things the last two years," his mother admitted. "I figured you wouldn't have a chance to meet anybody else locally, and I was hoping you would come back to live here."

He slowly shook his head. "The only reason I'll come back and live here is if I don't enjoy my job in Texas anymore," he said slowly. "And that won't happen for quite a while."

"But, if you loved somebody here," his mother argued, "then maybe you'd come back and find work here."

This was a side of his mother he had never seen before. "I'm surprised to hear that," he said slowly, not sure how to proceed. He didn't want to add to her pain, but he'd never heard anything even remotely as loving as this from her. "Why did you care?"

She flushed. "I get that you have seen me as a not very caring mother," she admitted painfully, "but I've always loved you."

He shared a glance with his father. "What brought this on?"

She shrugged helplessly. "I don't know," she said, "but … maybe suddenly seeing how much Reana was like me? She was a very difficult person sometimes. And I know I haven't been very easy to live with." She glanced apologetically up at her husband and then over at her son. "Like seeing a mirror image of myself. One of those snapshots of awareness and I thought, well, maybe I could do something to help Reana too. I wanted to talk to her about not attacking you. First time she sees you in two years, and she walks up in a public place—our family's business—and slaps you hard. I never did get a chance to tell you how much I admired the fact that you didn't turn around and belt her one. I know that's not what I said at the time because I wanted you to stop her, but you couldn't be the one to hit her," she said painfully. "Honestly I'm the one who should have. It would take another woman to hit her back, and it's probably the only way she'd ever stop. She was becoming more abusive in so many ways, and I guess that's what I saw in myself."

"She *was* more abusive," Raina said quietly from his side, "because she was so unhappy with who she was. She truly loved Jenny. Jenny wanted to go public with their relationship, and Reana didn't think she could handle how people would look at her—would judge her. She wasn't ready to take that step. Yet, she really wanted to be with Jenny. Apparently Reana was a completely different person when she was around Jenny."

"I could see that," Annemarie said. "I wish she'd told us though."

"It wouldn't have mattered to me," Harold said. "I was happy with her being herself. I didn't care what her sexual orientation was."

"No, and maybe I would have understood the breakup more," Annemarie said. She glanced up at Reyes. "She kept telling me how she caught you in bed with another woman."

"That's because she didn't want you to know the truth," Reyes said. "The fact is, I found Reana and Jenny in bed together. I didn't know her name at the time. It was a newish relationship, I believe, for them."

"She was with Jenny even way back then?" Harold asked in surprise. "She dated a lot of guys after you left."

"All part of that mixed-up persona of who she was trying to portray versus who she was," Raina said sadly. "What I don't understand is who, in the final moments of her life, was pissed off enough about that to kill her."

"Can you know for sure that's what it was about?" Harold asked. He glanced at Annemarie. "And where and when did you see her?"

"I saw her at the brownstone. I got there just as she was walking up the stairs."

Reyes straightened. "Did you talk inside or outside?"

"Outside on the front step. She said she had somebody inside waiting for her and wouldn't invite me in. And I was okay with that. But I wanted her to stop her abuse. I wanted her to treat you nicely. What can I say? It was something I finally felt I had to do."

"And did she just agree and go inside?"

His mother laughed. "No." There was bitterness in her voice. "I got really angry, and I smacked her."

# Chapter 16

RAINA STUDIED ANNEMARIE in horror. "You do realize I saw that smack on her face at the morgue right?"

Annemarie's eyes filled with tears. "You said she was beaten up, and I was terrified that that's what you meant." She shuddered, wrapping her arms tight around her chest. "I swear to you. I only hit her once."

"How many times have I told you that you've got to stop lashing out at people? Verbally is bad enough but physically?" Harold said, his voice harsher than Raina had ever heard before.

Annemarie bit her lip. "I just lost my temper." She looked at each of them and turned. "Like Reana did when she saw you, Reyes."

"But that wasn't temper," Reyes said quietly. "It was fear. Is that why you hit her? Were you afraid of something she was doing?"

His mother swallowed hard.

He leaned forward and said, "This is the time to come clean."

"I was afraid she was stealing from the company," she said, the words coming out in a rush. "And I wanted to talk to her about it. But I was also so angry about how she treated you."

"I highly doubt she was stealing from us," Harold protested.

"It's just something she said. Something about Reyes *would pay for it*. That she'd make sure there was nothing for him at the end of the day."

"So not that she was stealing from you but that she might?" Raina asked. She frowned, thinking about her sister. "I do know that, when she was very angry—or as Reyes said, afraid—she would make a lot of threats. But I highly doubt she would have carried it out. It would have crippled her career."

"I know, but it was enough of a fear factor for me to go to her brownstone," Annemarie said. "However, I only hit her once, and, when I left, she was alive."

"Why did you go there?"

"I followed her from work," she confessed. "I didn't think anything of it. I just reacted."

"She lived with Jenny there," Reyes said quietly. "But these last few days, maybe even as long as a week after they broke up, she'd been staying with Melissa."

Annemarie looked at him in surprise. "Well, she walked from the street, up the stairs and had the keys in her hand."

"Jenny started moving out a week ago," Raina said. "She was hoping she and Reana would make up again, but it didn't happen."

"So when Reana went to the brownstone, no one was there?" Harold asked.

"Jenny was no longer living there," Reyes corrected. "But you said she was meeting someone inside?"

Annemarie nodded. "Yes, but I didn't see who it was."

"Reana didn't say anything?"

Annemarie shook her head. "No, she didn't. We talked, and she went inside and slammed the door in my face, and I stormed off."

Reyes studied her for a long moment. "Did you see any other vehicles around?"

"Of course," she said. "There were lots. But how would I know if any of them belonged to the guy or woman inside?"

"What vehicles did you see?"

She shrugged. "I remember a van and a sports car. But I don't remember much else."

"What kind of sports car?" Reyes asked, feeling Raina look at him with something akin to excitement. "What kind of sports car, Mom?"

"How would I know?" She gave a hard laugh. "I don't know anything about cars."

"Can you describe it?"

She thought about it for a moment and then opened her laptop. "Let me see if I can find a picture. Though I don't know if that'll help."

They waited as she searched on the internet for sports cars.

"Aha," she said, flipping the laptop around. "It was like this. But it was black."

Raina stared at it, turning to look at Reyes. "What kind of sports car does Jamie drive?"

"According to Ice, a Mitsubishi Spider," he said with a note of satisfaction. "That vehicle. And it's black."

"Who's Jamie?" Harold and Annemarie asked together.

"Jenny's brother," Raina said. "Now I think that moves him up our priority list."

"Let me contact the detective first," Reyes said.

REYES STEPPED OUT of his parents' office and got Detective

Burgess on the phone. "We think Jamie was the last one to see Reana before her death."

"Explain," he said.

Reyes told the detective about his mother's confession and about the fact that a Mitsubishi Spider was parked outside and about Reana's comment that she was meeting somebody inside the brownstone.

"We called Jamie today, but we didn't connect."

"Maybe you should do a home visit," Reyes said. "Not to mention, somebody needs to do a wellness check on Jenny."

He heard the detective suck back his breath. "Look. I'll get ahold of Jamie. Send a black-and-white to his place. You see if you can track down Jenny and get back to me."

"On it," Reyes said. He called Jenny, thankful Raina had asked for the number. When there was no answer, he frowned and dialed again.

"Still no answer." He called the detective back.

"And Jamie didn't go to work today," the detective said, his voice grim. "We're on this. You just stay out of the way now. We can't have you getting into the middle of an operation and getting shot."

Reyes snorted. "So far we're the ones who have found all the information."

"It doesn't matter," the detective said. "Time to back off."

When Reyes looked up from his phone, he saw Ice standing in front of him, a frown on her face.

"Did I just hear that last part?"

He filled her in on the rest.

"Sounds like we need to get some men there," Ice said.

"Sure, but the detective just warned us off."

She shrugged with an elegant movement that made Reyes smile. "First off, they have to figure out where Jenny and Jamie are. Do you have any idea?"

He thought about it and then nodded. "Maybe they're at Reana's brownstone."

Ice's eyes lit with understanding. "Follow me," she said, "and we'll contact the law on our way."

"I'll bring Raina," he said. "I don't know what shape Jenny is in."

Ice, almost ready to walk out the front door, turned back to look at him. "Do you think Jenny killed Reana?"

He wasn't surprised at the question. He'd had to consider it himself. Reyes answered honestly, "I have no idea. But she's certainly capable of it—everyone is. Particularly when it comes to love and passion."

On that note, Ice pivoted and walked out. Reyes turned to see Raina racing toward him. He held out his hand. She grabbed it, and he tucked her close and walked to the Jeep, explaining as they went.

"We're taking a hell of a chance that they're there," she noted. "We were just there ourselves."

"Sure," Reyes said. "But it's the one place we know to look for her. For all we know, they could have gone down to the beach. Maybe they were having lunch somewhere."

"Do you think Jenny killed Reana?" Her words echoed Ice's.

"No clue," he said, his tone hard. "For all I know, Jamie and Jenny were both in love with the same woman."

At that, Raina shut up in shocked silence.

# Chapter 17

RAINA HADN'T CONSIDERED that Jamie might also be in love with Reana. But, given Reana's history, it was quite possible. Raina would hope not. But it was anybody's guess. They were about fifteen minutes away with the traffic heavy. Ice drove ahead of them.

Raina glanced at Reyes. "Who's calling the detective?"

"I let Ice do it. She has more pull than I do." He gave Raina a crooked grin. "I was told to stay away."

"Sure, but you know how quickly the detectives will mobilize."

"You mean, how quickly they won't mobilize," he said. "They're sending in a black-and-white to Jamie's residence, his place of business and to the brownstone. But they won't get there fast enough. So we'll check it out. And, if we need to, we can always call them in for backup."

She shook her head. "I have a sinking feeling in my stomach that we should be calling for backup now," she said.

"In this case, we have something much better."

She glanced at him. "What?"

"Not *what*," he said. "Who. You haven't seen anyone in action until you've seen Ice move."

Just then his phone rang. He propped it up on the dash and hit Speaker, "Ice, what's up?"

"Both vehicles are here," she said. "I've called Detective

Burgess. You come around to the back and approach quietly. Make sure Raina stays in the vehicle."

Raina protested.

"Unless you're armed and ready for physical combat," Ice said, her voice hard, "you stay in the vehicle, and you stay hidden. Do you hear me?"

Raina winced. "Yes, ma'am." There was a bite to her tone.

At that, Ice chuckled. "Good. Glad to hear it." She hung up.

Raina stared at Reyes. "She's really a commander, isn't she?"

"You have no idea," he said. He followed Ice's instructions, pulling into the back alley, up against the fence. He took his keys, pocketed them, grabbed his cell phone and said, "Don't move." Then he reached across and pulled a handgun from the glove box.

She stared at it.

He just gave her a bland look. "Yes, I have a license." And then, just like that, he was gone.

She'd been ordered to stay. But it was pretty damn hard when she wouldn't know what was going on. She also didn't want to get caught in a vehicle by anybody running away.

On that thought, she hopped out and walked about ten to twenty feet, trying to peer through knotholes in the fence. All she could see was the neighbor's yard. Every one of these places had long narrow backyards, like little perfect rectangles. She went farther, looking for a knothole that would reveal her sister's backyard. There was one about two feet up from the ground. She bent, trying to see. It was hard though. She saw Reyes racing toward the back door, sliding along the fence. If she hadn't been looking for him, she didn't think she'd have seen him. And then suddenly he was at the kitchen door, peering in through the window of the door. Whatever he saw had him pulling out his handgun. All of a sudden he kicked down the door and entered.

"STOP," HE ROARED as he faced Jamie over his sister's body on the floor. "Put that weapon down."

And, sure enough, Jamie held the gun against his own sister. And that's when another truth came home. Their features were so similar, as in not just siblings but maybe twins?

And then Reyes knew for sure. "You loved her too, didn't you?"

Jamie wasn't willing to give an inch. His sister sobbed as she lay on the floor. "I love my sister," he said sarcastically. "Of course I do."

"But you loved Reana too, didn't you?" Reyes didn't know where Ice was, but he sure as hell hoped she was coming through the front door right now because he'd entered without backup. Rule number one was to let the rest of your team know your actions. But, once he'd seen Jamie put the gun against Jenny's head, Reyes had to act.

"Yes," Jamie said defiantly. His hand was steady, his trigger finger shifting ever-so-slightly.

"Don't do it," Reyes said. "You might have loved the same woman, but that's no reason to hurt your sister."

"If it hadn't been for her, Reana would be with me."

"And, if it hadn't been for you," Jenny said with spirit, looking up at her brother, "she'd be with me today."

Jamie sneered. "All she needed was a good man. That's the way things should be. It's the natural order of things."

Reyes shook his head. "You just don't get it, do you? It had nothing to do with sex. It had everything to do with love. And she loved your sister. She didn't love you."

Jamie's temper rose, and the look in his eyes turned glacial.

Slowly, ever-so-slowly, Reyes started to pull the trigger on his gun. "You do not want to fire that gun," he said. "Because I'll take you out, and I won't miss."

Jamie laughed. "I don't give a shit. Reana is gone. I killed her. I didn't want to. But the stupid bitch laughed at me. She told me how much she loved my sister and how much she hated me. She used me," he cried out passionately. "You know what that's like?"

Inside Reyes winced because he did know exactly what that was like.

"I would have driven her to my sister's place, so she'd be the one to find Reana's body, then couldn't take the chance after a cop drove past, looking at me. I dumped Reana in her vehicle behind a coffee shop and hoofed it back to my car."

Reyes was also delighted that Jamie hadn't followed through on that plan. Such a discovery would only have added to Jenny's pain. "I do know what it is like to be one of Reana's rejects," he said. "I was her fiancé a couple years ago."

Jamie narrowed his gaze at him. "You?" he asked, his tone incredulous.

Reyes deliberately didn't let him get his goat. "Yeah, me," he said in a conversational tone.

"No way." Jamie seemed to consider it, then shook his head. "Even if you were, she didn't care. It's her sister she kept trying to call while I toyed with her. I let her think she'd get a call through, then stopped it. Would hit Redial in front of Reana's face, then shut it off. She knew I was serious. And I was—fucking serious." His voice rose with anger as he contemplated his sister. "She didn't call *you*. So you see? Reana didn't love you. She loved me."

Behind Jamie, Reyes saw Ice motioning on the floor at Jenny. Finally Jenny saw her. She turned her head and frowned. Reyes wasn't sure exactly what instructions Ice was trying to give to Jenny. Reyes didn't dare take his gaze off the man holding the gun.

"I'm sorry you killed her," Reyes said. "Reana was finally coming into herself. Finally understanding who and what she wanted."

"She was a fucking lesbo," Jamie said. "Just look at my sister. You know what it's like growing up with a twin, knowing exactly what each other is thinking and doing? And then to see that her sexual orientation was so twisted?"

"Why did you care?" Reyes said. "Reana and Jenny were happy together. Nothing else mattered."

"Sure it matters," Jamie said. "It matters to me." And he smiled and tightened his trigger finger, his gaze strong and never leaving Reyes's.

Reyes's response was immediate. He took one shot, and he didn't miss.

As Jamie fell to the floor, Jenny burst out crying. Ice was suddenly at her side. Ice and Reyes exchanged hard looks, whereas Jenny was a balled-up mess, sobbing as she crawled to her brother. She turned to look up at Reyes. "Did you have to kill him?"

"Yes," Ice said firmly. "If not him, it would have been you killed by your own brother."

Jenny nodded and collapsed into Ice's arms. Reyes noted Raina looking in the kitchen window. He walked over to the kitchen door, opened it and snapped at her, "You were supposed to stay in the vehicle."

She shrugged and stepped into his arms. "I saw you busting in the door, and I knew things would get ugly."

"What would you do about it?" he asked in outrage.

She leaned back and looked at him. "I don't know what I would have done, but I would have done something. So, if you're done yelling at me, I suggest you get something to cover up this piece of shit on the floor and call an ambulance for Jenny. She'll need some help."

The two of them glared at each other for a moment, until Reyes just chuckled, held her tight and then kissed her hard and passionately.

When the hot and heavy kiss ended, she sagged against him, while he pulled out his phone and called the detective.

As soon as the detective answered, Reyes said, "Send an ambulance. Reana's killer is dead, and his twin sister has been beaten."

"Did you kill him?" The detective's voice rose.

"Absolutely," Reyes said. "It was either that or let him kill his sister. He was doing exactly the same thing he'd done to Reana. He'd beaten Jenny up first and was standing there, holding a gun to her head."

"Don't you move," the detective said. "I'll be there in twenty."

"No hurry now," Reyes said. "The danger is over. Now there's just a hell of a lot of healing that needs to take place."

# Chapter 18

I T WAS LATE in the afternoon when Ice led Reyes and Raina into her father's house. Raina stopped and stared. "This is stunning. And to think Reyes spent the night at my place on a small couch last night," she joked.

Reyes wrapped an arm around her shoulders, kissed her hard and said, "Well, tonight you can stay here with me."

"I'm so exhausted," she said. "I'm almost ready for bed now."

In front of her stood a man with silver hair in a distinguished suit, smiling at them. "Hopefully you can make it through another hour or two. We're just getting dinner ready. And we're about to open a bottle of wine. Time to relax, eat and then you can rest, my dear."

She smiled, stepped forward and tried to shake his hand. But he wouldn't have anything to do with it.

He wrapped his arms around her. "I'm so sorry for the horrible couple days you've had."

Tears coming to her eyes, she stepped back and smiled at him. "Isn't that the truth? I hope to never again experience such a terrible time."

They were led into a massive kitchen, where another man puttered around. She was introduced to him and then a glass of red wine was put in her hand, and she was led outside beside a pool and what appeared to be huge palm trees. She wandered the garden, trying to let the stress drop off her. Reyes, as always, was there, walking quietly at her side.

"Are you still okay to stay for a few days?" she murmured.

"I am," he said. "We'll take care of the final duties to your mother and sister, and we might have to help Jenny with Jamie."

Raina winced at that. But she understood Jenny would have a hard time burying her twin too. "Hopefully she has family still."

"We'll check," he said. They walked to the end of the garden out of earshot from the others. He stopped and turned her to face him. "And then I want you to think about something else."

She looked up at him. "What?"

"I want you to consider returning to Texas with me."

Her jaw dropped. "Are you serious?"

"I'm very serious," he said. "Nothing is left for you here. It's a clean start—in Texas, with me. I don't know what you want to do with your life, but I know Ice could certainly use some help with all the transplanting."

That startled a laugh out of her. "Wow. I hadn't expected that." And she hadn't, but she'd certainly hoped maybe something like that could happen down the road. "Isn't it too fast?" she asked with a bit of worry.

"No," he said, "it isn't. We've had this coming for a long time."

She smiled and kissed him gently on the lips. "You have to ask Ice's permission."

He chuckled. "I already have."

Raina smiled at Ice.

Ice lifted her glass of wine, as if in cheers.

And Raina realized Ice really did approve. "Are you sure?" she fiercely asked Reyes. "Because, when you say, yes, you can't take it back."

He chuckled. "I have no intention of taking anything back," he whispered. He tilted her chin and kissed her gently. "That's a kiss of promise. We'll handle everything here as much as we can. I can't stay away too long, but we have several full days to get through here. Then I want you to take that leap of faith and come live with me in Texas. Together we'll grow and learn and build a future for just us. Leave all this pain behind so we can both live in the sunshine."

She smiled up at him mistily. "I haven't heard a better proposition ever in my life."

He chuckled. "Let's just hope that's the only one you ever hear." He wrapped his arm around her and pulled her gently into his arms. "It'll be good," he whispered. "You'll see."

She tilted her head back and whispered, "I already know. It won't be just good. It'll be great."

# Epilogue

DEZI ARNETT COULDN'T wait for Ice to show up. She'd flown into the Houston airport about an hour ago. They'd sent several trucks to help offload the plane. One truck had already arrived at the compound, driven by Anders, while Harrison followed in the company vehicle. Everybody on hand at the compound helped to unload the first truck, knowing a second was due any moment at the compound with even more plants. Driving this final load would be Reyes, accompanied by Ice, Vince, and Reyes's new girlfriend, Raina. Dezi had been teasing Reyes by text ever since finding out the news.

When the second truck finally pulled into the gate, Dezi stopped and stared as the people exited. Raina's auburn hair was in long waves, reaching her midback. She was slim, a hint of freckles across her peaches-and-cream skin. She never looked at anyone but Reyes. Dezi stopped and stared, shaking his head.

Stone walked up and nudged him. "You're next," he said with a fat grin.

Dezi shook his head. "If you could find me another one of those, hell yes," he said fervently. "But I never seem to find them myself." There was real sorrow in his voice. "Reyes said it wouldn't happen for him, but ..."

"Yeah. You see? He went with Ice. That's a guarantee

it'll happen. So the next time Ice is looking for a volunteer to go on a mission, you might want to be the one who steps up to the plate."

Dezi tossed Stone a look. "Yeah, but she travels all over the world. You don't find girls like this everywhere."

Stone's grin flashed. "No, but Ice knows how to find the diamonds in the world. She may have had to go to California for Reyes to find his, but you can bet one's out there for you too."

Dezi shook his head. "Hell no. All I ever see is a lot of uncut gems or really high rollers who need fancy settings to keep them happy."

At that, Stone laughed. "That's pretty funny," he said. "But ye of little faith don't understand the magic that's Levi and Ice."

"Oh, I *see* the magic," Dezi said. "I see it all the time. With every frickin' one of you."

"Sure," Stone said, "and you're the next one to find it."

Just then Dezi watched as Vince got out of the vehicle behind Reyes and Raina. The three were laughing. "I see Ice decided to hire Vince too?"

"Absolutely," Stone said. "We're always shorthanded. You know that."

"Yeah. You see though," Dezi said with a fat grin, "Vince is single."

Stone turned to look at the new arrival with an assessing gaze. "Ice will hook him up in no time too."

"He'll be next," Dezi said. "Not me. I don't have that kind of luck."

Stone laughed. "You don't understand," he said. "Luck has nothing to do with it. It's all about Ice. Don't you worry, Dezi. She'll find a diamond just for you."

But Dezi wasn't convinced. Still, he looked at Reyes and Raina coming toward him. Dezi wondered if that kind of love was possible for him.

This concludes Book 17 of Heroes for Hire: Reyes's Raina.

Read about Dezi's Diamond: Heroes for Hire, Book 18

# Heroes for Hire: Dezi's Diamond (Book #18)

**When opposites attract... anything can happen...**

Dezi was a plain-and-simple type of guy. He loved working for Levi's company and had enjoyed the jobs he'd been given so far. When a businesswoman contacted Ice over, well, ice, ... things got interesting.

Diamond was an exclusive jewelry designer, born and raised in the industry, working within her father's diamond company. When a custom-designed item was checked before shipment, she realized the piece wasn't her workmanship. Somehow someone had forged her work and had slipped it in the shipment as a replacement.

However, the theft and forgery quickly escalate to kidnapping and armed robbery. Dezi and Diamond need to figure this out fast, before something else gets added to the list: murder.

Book 18 is available now!

To find out more visit Dale Mayer's website.

http://smarturl.it/DMDeziUniversal

# Author's Note

Thank you for reading Reyes's Raina: Heroes for Hire, Book 17! If you enjoyed the book, please take a moment and leave a short review.

Dear reader,

I love to hear from readers, and you can contact me at my website: www.dalemayer.com or at my Facebook author page. To be informed of new releases and special offers, sign up for my newsletter or follow me on BookBub. And if you are interested in joining Dale Mayer's Reader Group, here is the Facebook sign up page.
facebook.com/groups/402384989872660

Cheers,
Dale Mayer

# Your Free Book Awaits!

### *KILL OR BE KILLED*

Part of an elite SEAL team, Mason takes on the dangerous jobs no one else wants to do – or can do. When he's on a mission, he's focused and dedicated. When he's not, he plays as hard as he fights.

Until he meets a woman he can't have but can't forget. Software developer, Tesla lost her brother in combat and has no intention of getting close to someone else in the military. Determined to save other US soldiers from a similar fate, she's created a program that could save lives. But other countries know about the program, and they won't stop until they get it – and get her.

*Time is running out ... For her ... For him ... For them ...*

**DOWNLOAD** a *__complimentary__* copy of MASON? Just tell me where to send it!

http://dalemayer.com/sealsmason/

# About the Author

Dale Mayer is a USA Today bestselling author best known for her Psychic Visions and Family Blood Ties series. Her contemporary romances are raw and full of passion and emotion (Second Chances, SKIN), her thrillers will keep you guessing (By Death series), and her romantic comedies will keep you giggling (It's a Dog's Life and Charmin Marvin Romantic Comedy series).

She honors the stories that come to her – and some of them are crazy and break all the rules and cross multiple genres!

To go with her fiction, she also writes nonfiction in many different fields with books available on resume writing, companion gardening and the US mortgage system. She has recently published her Career Essentials Series. All her books are available in print and ebook format.

## Connect with Dale Mayer Online

*Dale's Website – www.dalemayer.com*
*Twitter – @DaleMayer*
*Facebook – dalemayer.com/fb*
*BookBub – bookbub.com/authors/dale-mayer*

# Also by Dale Mayer

## Published Adult Books:

### Lovely Lethal Gardens

Arsenic in the Azaleas, Book 1

Bones in the Begonias, Book 2

Corpse in the Carnations, Book 3

Daggers in the Dahlias, Book 4

Evidence in the Echinacea, Book 5

Footprints in the Ferns, Book 6

### Psychic Vision Series

Tuesday's Child

Hide 'n Go Seek

Maddy's Floor

Garden of Sorrow

Knock Knock...

Rare Find

Eyes to the Soul

Now You See Her

Shattered

Into the Abyss

Seeds of Malice

Eye of the Falcon

Itsy-Bitsy Spider

Unmasked

Deep Beneath

Psychic Visions Books 1–3

Psychic Visions Books 4–6

Psychic Visions Books 7–9

## By Death Series

Touched by Death

Haunted by Death

Chilled by Death

By Death Books 1–3

## Broken Protocols – Romantic Comedy Series

Cat's Meow

Cat's Pajamas

Cat's Cradle

Cat's Claus

Broken Protocols 1-4

## Broken and... Mending

Skin

Scars

Scales (of Justice)

Broken but... Mending 1-3

## Glory

Genesis

Tori

Celeste

Glory Trilogy

## Biker Blues

Morgan: Biker Blues, Volume 1

Cash: Biker Blues, Volume 2

## SEALs of Honor

Mason: SEALs of Honor, Book 1

Hawk: SEALs of Honor, Book 2

Dane: SEALs of Honor, Book 3

Swede: SEALs of Honor, Book 4

Shadow: SEALs of Honor, Book 5

Cooper: SEALs of Honor, Book 6

Markus: SEALs of Honor, Book 7

Evan: SEALs of Honor, Book 8

Mason's Wish: SEALs of Honor, Book 9

Chase: SEALs of Honor, Book 10

Brett: SEALs of Honor, Book 11

Devlin: SEALs of Honor, Book 12

Easton: SEALs of Honor, Book 13

Ryder: SEALs of Honor, Book 14

Macklin: SEALs of Honor, Book 15

Corey: SEALs of Honor, Book 16

Warrick: SEALs of Honor, Book 17

Tanner: SEALs of Honor, Book 18

Jackson: SEALs of Honor, Book 19

Kanen: SEALs of Honor, Book 20

SEALs of Honor, Books 1–3

SEALs of Honor, Books 4–6

SEALs of Honor, Books 7–10

SEALs of Honor, Books 11–13

SEALs of Honor, Books 14–16

SEALs of Honor, Books 17–19

## Heroes for Hire

Levi's Legend: Heroes for Hire, Book 1

Stone's Surrender: Heroes for Hire, Book 2

Merk's Mistake: Heroes for Hire, Book 3

Rhodes's Reward: Heroes for Hire, Book 4

Flynn's Firecracker: Heroes for Hire, Book 5

Logan's Light: Heroes for Hire, Book 6

Harrison's Heart: Heroes for Hire, Book 7

Saul's Sweetheart: Heroes for Hire, Book 8

Dakota's Delight: Heroes for Hire, Book 9

Michael's Mercy (Part of Sleeper SEAL Series)

Tyson's Treasure: Heroes for Hire, Book 10

Jace's Jewel: Heroes for Hire, Book 11

Rory's Rose: Heroes for Hire, Book 12

Brandon's Bliss: Heroes for Hire, Book 13

Liam's Lily: Heroes for Hire, Book 14

North's Nikki: Heroes for Hire, Book 15

Anders's Angel: Heroes for Hire, Book 16

Reyes's Raina: Heroes for Hire, Book 17

Dezi's Diamond: Heroes for Hire, Book 18

Vince's Vixen: Heroes for Hire, Book 19

Heroes for Hire, Books 1–3

Heroes for Hire, Books 4–6

Heroes for Hire, Books 7–9

## SEALs of Steel

Badger: SEALs of Steel, Book 1
Erick: SEALs of Steel, Book 2
Cade: SEALs of Steel, Book 3
Talon: SEALs of Steel, Book 4
Laszlo: SEALs of Steel, Book 5
Geir: SEALs of Steel, Book 6
Jager: SEALs of Steel, Book 7
The Last Wish: SEALs of Steel, Book 8

## Collections

Dare to Be You…
Dare to Love…
Dare to be Strong…
RomanceX3

## Standalone Novellas

It's a Dog's Life
Riana's Revenge
Second Chances

# Published Young Adult Books:

## Family Blood Ties Series

Vampire in Denial
Vampire in Distress
Vampire in Design
Vampire in Deceit
Vampire in Defiance

Vampire in Conflict

Vampire in Chaos

Vampire in Crisis

Vampire in Control

Vampire in Charge

Family Blood Ties Set 1–3

Family Blood Ties Set 1–5

Family Blood Ties Set 4–6

Family Blood Ties Set 7–9

Sian's Solution, A Family Blood Ties Series Prequel Novelette

## Design series

Dangerous Designs

Deadly Designs

Darkest Designs

Design Series Trilogy

## Standalone

In Cassie's Corner

Gem Stone (a Gemma Stone Mystery)

Time Thieves

# Published Non-Fiction Books:

## Career Essentials

Career Essentials: The Résumé

Career Essentials: The Cover Letter

Career Essentials: The Interview

Career Essentials: 3 in 1

72354541R00136

Made in the
USA
Middletown, DE